The Red Rocks

Elizabeth Povarova-Simpson

This book is a work of fiction. Any references to historical events, real people or real places are used fictitiously. Other names, characters, places, and events are products of the author's imagination, and any resemblance to actual events or persons, living or dead, is entirely coincidental.

Copyright © 2017 by Elizabeth Povarova-Simpson

All rights reserved, including the right to reproduce this book or portions thereof in any form whatsoever.

Cover Illustration by Jamie Hibdon
Editing by Doug Harrison
Draft Reading by Josh Louder

First Edition October 2017
ISBN: 978-0-9994719-0-6

Dedicated to my wonderful husband Brent. Thank you for always standing by my side and encouraging me to keep writing. I love you, and I could've never done this without you.

&

Dedicated to my mom and dad. Thank you for the constant love and support. I love you very much.

PART I

August 2060 – Present Day
Jake Deen – The Red Rocks
Near Gerlach, Nevada

Jake opened one eye, slowly coming to, after a night of . . . *A night of what?* Jake felt a surge of panic. He couldn't remember a thing. He rolled over onto his back, looked from one side to the other, but saw only a crow on the ground, three vultures circling overhead, and the desert around him.

Stuck in the middle of nowhere again! He kicked the ground with his sockless heel, sending sprinkles of earth flying in the air. *Damn Red Rocks!—Fuck this post-2040 wasteland. No electricity, no phones, no GPS—what had the government been thinking?!*

Jake gulped in a mouthful of hot air, and then spit, trying to expel the stale-alcohol taste eroding his tongue. Let's piece this back together, he thought. He stuck out his hand to push himself up and winced as it landed on something sharp. He turned his head; it was a pocket knife. The orange bone handle told him it was his. He picked it up and wiped the dust off with a finger—the glare from the blade nearly blinded him. He squeezed his eyes shut seeing spots.

When his eyes adjusted, in the reflection he saw his light-colored hair caked into a single dreadlock, and his normally bright green eyes, dull, housing pinpoint pupils. A violet stain had crept into the furrow next to his snot-crusted nose.

Disgusted with himself, he pushed his meager weight up off the dry soil, his lungs barely allowing him to take a full breath, his head spinning like a carousel. At least his hat would keep him from getting heatstroke. He ran his fingers over it. *Is it mine though?* He took it off and examined it. Nope, he concluded, grimacing at the hot pink velvet. This neon fashion statement was wet in one spot.

Jake felt the back of his head. Blood. *Goddamn it. Drunk and blacked out again. Where the fuck am I? What the fuck happened?*

As he gauged the severity of the cut, his fingers touched an old scar. He recalled waking up one night to piles of bloody bandages sprawled out on the floor. His father didn't tell him what happened, but his gut told him the blow came from a belt—the one his father liked so much. *He didn't even stay with me while they stitched me up. It's a blessing he sent me away. Who knows what would've happened to me if I stayed?*

Jake pushed the memory away and focused on the matter at hand. He searched his jean pockets for clues, but all he found was a broken pack of cigarettes, a few Red Rock notes, and some matches from Johnny's Tavern, where men went for cheap beer and loose women. All Jake had done was make out with some blonde. Everything had been fine until that toothless asshole hit him with brass knuckles. In a fair fight, he could've taken him.

Jake stretched and felt pain all over his body. He couldn't begin to count the number of bruises. Despite a desire to lie back down on the dirt, he knew he needed to start moving. The sun looked like it was about noon, so he had time to make some headway before nightfall. Now, which way?

Jake stood, a mosaic of mud cracks decorated the hardpan beneath him. He was used to being on the road, so he could tell by his boot's shadow—stretching several feet away from him—which way was north. He looked for a landmark. Desert north, desert south, desert east, and desert west. *Fuck!* He surveyed his surroundings again, but the mountain silhouettes all looked the same through his blurry vision. I need water, he thought as sweat poured down his face. He started south, one step at a time, with labored breath. His sinewy body fought against him.

He passed an abandoned encampment of small, cone-roofed tents. Each was covered with aluminum foil and padded by layers of alkali dust. He scrounged for supplies, but found nothing except for a few empty waterskins and a sweater, which he wrapped around his waist. He kept on walking.

After about an hour, he saw a figure riding toward him out of the horizon's warbling haze. Jake slowed.

The rider approached and Jake's eyes swept the ground for anything he could use as a weapon, his knife being too small and dull.

"Hey!" the rider called out. Even from twenty feet away, the voice rang out strong. He was taller and bigger built than Jake, with dark hair, a cowboy hat, and a faded blue bandana covering his nose and mouth. He sat on a charcoal black mustang with a shiny coat, a sign of wealth in the Red Rocks.

"Hey," Jake answered, his voice coarse.

"What you up to in these parts?" The rider was eyeing Jake's velvet hat.

"Tryin' to get somewhere where I can get cleaned up." Jake took the hat off and put it behind his back. He noticed the rider's gun belt and tensed up.

"Are you asking for a ride?" The stranger cocked a thick brown eyebrow at Jake.

"I wasn't going to," Jake said. He was flexing and squinting, trying to look intimidating. *I probably look like a beat up asshole*, he thought.

The rider was studying Jake. "You have any currency?" he asked after a while.

"Not much." Jake looked down, feeling his cheeks grow warm. "Not much at all."

The rider looked off and spat. "Perhaps I can still help you. I'm headed to the next town east—Livingsworth. Some still call it Eureka, as it was called before 8/6/2040—before the Red Rocks were created. You know it?"

"I've heard of it, but never been there. The last place I visited was Gerlach."

"You're about twenty miles northeast of Gerlach right now," the rider said.

Jake touched his chin thoughtfully. That meant he'd probably ridden off on a horse last night and then lost it or got jumped. Wouldn't be the first time, he thought.

"Either way, do you want my help or not? Livingsworth is about one week's ride away. I can take you there." A strong wind blew and a small dust devil began to form beside them.

"I'd be stupid to say no."

"What's your name?" the rider asked. His horse shifted impatiently, reacting to the growing whirlwind and puffs of hot air coming their way.

"Jake."

"I'm Bill." The rider gave a nod with his hat. "Well, get on, Jake, before you keel over."

"Thanks, I really appreciate this," Jake said and got on. The horse neighed as he adjusted to the extra weight, and then they were off.

A fucking miracle, Jake thought, unless of course the guy was the rumored lone bandit that tied people up and then decapitated them. Jake put his hand in the pocket where his knife was; his heart pounded and breath shortened.

"Long night?" the man interrupted Jake's spiraling thoughts.

"You could say that." Jake coughed.

"Let me know if you need me to stop, as I prefer you don't vomit on my horse."

They rode in silence, the quiet broken only by the horse's hooves beating rhythmically against the ground. The terrain was vast and empty; its heat enveloped them, drying out their lungs and roasting any exposed skin. A wall of dust grew behind them—a wave ready to tip at the crest. Bill quickened their pace.

Jake felt filthy. He smelled like an overripe basket of fruit with his sweat-soaked T-shirt and beer-stained jeans. He was still drunk and the rough ride was making him queasy. *I can handle myself, I can keep it in.* The horse jerked as it stepped over a hidden rock. *Maybe not!*

He leaned over the side of the horse as hot putrid acid shot out of his mouth and nose.

"Get off." Bill nudged him.

Jake jumped off, then he squatted, heaving until his stomach had nothing more.

"Take this." Bill handed Jake a black pill and a canteen of water. Jake didn't ask what the pill was. He didn't care. A light fizzing sound came from inside his mouth before he swallowed it. He poured the rest of the water on his face.

Bill glanced at Jake, annoyed. "We needed that water." His tone was stern, but not loud, like when a father scolds his child without raising his voice.

Oh no. "Shit, I didn't mean to I—"

"Just get on."

A few minutes later, as they rode at a slower pace, Jake yawned and his eyelids closed.

Did he dose me with something? Disturbing thoughts pecked their way into his fuzzy mind, reminding him of the rumored lone bandit. And then, complete darkness.

August 2060 – Present Day
Jake Deen – The Red Rocks
Road to Livingsworth, Nevada

"Hey." Bill tugged on Jake's shirt. "We've stopped for the night."

Jake rubbed his eyes and saw that they were no longer on the flat, clay-wrapped crust of the desert, but surrounded by golden hills, dotted with dried-out weeds. The clouds reminded him of accordion bellows, they opened up to let out a soundless tune.

Still got my head, Jake thought. He smiled to himself while he yawned. He felt rested, but his head was pounding like a hammer on a railroad spike.

"Feeling better from the charcoal?" Bill asked. "It should've absorbed some of the toxins."

"Not 100 percent."

"Tough to get back to 100 percent, after a glut of alcohol."

Indeed it is, Jake thought, then shrugged. I've come back from worse.

Bill handed him a pouch. "Here's some flint. Can you prep and start a fire?"

"Sure." Jake staggered off in search of rocks to create a pit. There was no wind, no birds; only silence, but for a light scuttle of insects. The darkness was taking over daylight, and he hurried to pick up as many stones as he could find, trying his best to avoid the feisty succulents poking out in thorned bouquets.

"Damn!" A pinpricked pain shot through Jake's arm and he dropped the rocks he was cradling. He looked down and saw the eight-legged culprit crawl away. His hand cramped and he returned to the spot where they planned to set up camp. A swell began to form around a red dot on his palm and his whole body began to throb.

"What happened to your hand?" Bill appeared as if out of nowhere, startling Jake.

Jake took a deep breath. "I think a spider bit me."

Bill took Jake's hand and shook his head. He pulled him over to his horse, took out a solar-powered flash light from his satchel, and turned it on, focusing the beam on Jakes' palm.

"Looks like a Red Rocks widow bite," Bill confirmed.

Jake gulped. "Isn't it deadly?"

"Sometimes." Bill took out a glass tube, a razor and bandage out of the same leather satchel.

He grabbed a hunter's knife from his belt and cut into the meat of Jake's palm, leaving a red, wet trail. Jake fought to keep a steady hand, his instincts telling him to pull away. He noticed that Bill seemed unnerved by the process.

Jake cringed as Bill dropped several milligrams of purple liquid into his fresh cut. Then he dressed Jake's wound with the netted white cloth. Jake felt a cooling sensation creep its way into his hand, and his pain subsided.

"Sit here. Try not to get your heart rate up. I'll prep the camp."

"Okay," Jake said. I won't argue with that, he thought.

An hour later, Jake stared into the fire and chewed on bread and hard cheese. The pops and cracks of the flames set a beat to an unknown song; the smell of burned wood offered comfort. He looked at Bill, who was rationing out the remaining dried meat and fruit into six piles. Before wrapping each portion in paper, he added an oblong gummy to each. Jake leaned over for a closer look.

"Red Rocks pellets," Bill said. "They don't taste good, but they provide a full day's nourishment for an active male adult."

Jake nodded. This guy knows what he is doing, he thought. Tent, food, flint, extra horseshoes, and now pellets? It wasn't his first time on the road, that was for sure. It looked like he was carrying some other stuff as well. Jake was eyeing the satchels on each side of the horse. He wondered if there was something in there that could knock this hangover out for good: liquor, grass, more of those charcoal sleeping pills? All three if he was lucky. Jake smiled at the thought, but then worry crossed his face. What if the guy was carrying something he wasn't supposed to, and they ran into someone they weren't supposed to: scavengers, gangs, or even worse—a marshal?

Bill looked up as if he'd heard Jake's thoughts. He held Jake's gaze across the fire. His nose and mouth, now free from the bandana, showed sharp features with a prominent chin.

"So . . ." Jake started, breaking the silence, but then he hesitated.

"So what?" Bill's deep voice vibrated against the shadowy hills.

Jake reached to smooth out his hair, but then remembered it was knotted and stopped himself. He cleared his throat and asked, "Why did you stop for me anyway?"

"It was not the smartest idea, considering you could be dangerous. Or crazy." Bill shrugged. "What would *you* have done?"

"Probably not stop," Jake said.

"Your hat made you look less threatening," Bill joked.

Jake blushed, thinking about what he must've looked like—a swollen face with a neon pink topper.

Bill finished off his bread and took out a tobacco pouch and papers.

"So, how long have you been in the Red Rocks?" Jake asked the most commonly asked question in the Red Rocks.

"Ten years," Bill said without looking up. "And you?"

"About that and a half. Do you ever go back?" Jake asked.

Bill looked away. Then he took off his cowboy hat and placed it on the ground next to where he was sitting. Jake noticed the streaks of gray in Bill's hair. He was ten or fifteen years older than Jake.

"There's nothing left for me in the Metropolitans." Bill paused, then said, "I prefer the simplicity of the Red Rocks to the chaos of big city life."

Jake nodded. "I hear it's still wild out there, worse than before 8/6/2040. Can't move an inch without being accosted by all of the lights and noise. Fucking ads everywhere."

"And you?"

"I didn't leave by choice. My father sent me away." Jake shivered, although it wasn't cold. He looked up at the sky, now lit with countless stars. A lonely howl conjured the image of a coyote standing, conversing with the moon.

Bill nodded, hair falling over dark, understanding eyes.

The men sat in silence for several minutes, each in their own distant memories.

"Let's get the rest of our sleeping gear." Bill stood up, brushed off his jeans, and headed off to grab the blankets. Jake followed to help him out, once more admiring Bill's skilled approach to setting up camp. It looked like his whole life was on that horse. Better than Jake's life, stumbling from one town to the next with barely enough money to eat, sleep, and now without even a horse to ride.

August 2060 – Present Day
Bill Vos – The Red Rocks
Road to Livingsworth, Nevada

Bill and Jake rode for the next three days, not a soul in sight. They spoke only when necessary, keeping their focus and energy on the road.

On day four, running low on water, they crossed the highway to get to the river. Green sprouts poked through cracks that zigzagged through the gray cement. Horseshit, old canteens, and animal bones were scattered on the sides. Bill hated highways, finding it safer to follow the same route a few miles out.

They made their way down a rocky hill to the river and found it dry. Bill knew it would be, but he had to try for Jake, not because he felt sorry for him, but because . . . he didn't know why. He just had a feeling about Jake, a sort of familiarity. They would have to ration what they had left. Travel less during the heat. Wet their lips only if they needed to.

On day five, Bill began to worry. The heat exhaustion and the Red Rocks widow's poison was getting to Jake. He had not stopped talking. Bill lined Jake's hat with cooling bandages and told him not to take it off.

"You know Bill, you have it all together. I have nothing together. I think you know how to live. You know how to do everything right. What do I know about life bouncing from place to place and nowhere to call home? Do you have a home?"

Bill sighed knowing Jake wasn't looking for a response.

"And you know what else? Have you ever wondered why there is no 's' on the Red Rock notes? I heard the Treasury Department forgot to add the 's' in the first print. Then they were like 'fuck it, no one will notice' and just kept printing the notes. What a jo—Is that a rabbit?"

Bill looked over at the crumbly tree stump Jake was pointing to. "No." He cleared his throat.

"Damn. Oh well. Anyway, you know what else?"

Bill clenched his teeth.

"I was so young when they sent me away, and my mom, oh god I loved my mom."

"Shhh," Bill said and pointed at crisscrossing sticks protruding from a conical top of a structure, the rest of which was hidden by a cluster of shrubs.

"What's that?" Jake asked, his voice bubbly like a child's.

"Let's go take a look," said Bill. They slipped off the horse and Bill grabbed Jake's arm. "Carefully and quietly," he warned.

They walked through the wiry grass, its blades jabbing and scratching through threadbare jeans. As they got closer, Bill put his hand down to his leather gun belt.

If it's abandoned, let's hope there's water, Bill thought. If not . . . Bill bent a tree branch out of his way, and a few leaves fell to the ground. *Crack!* The branch broke and a startled deer ran off to find shady cover.

"Shit!" Bill said. "Come on." He motioned for Jake to follow him. Through the brush, was a small clearing with stomped-down turf, and a rawhide tipi surrounded by wooden poles. The crunching sounds of dried grass crumpling and twigs breaking droned from the bushes behind the tipi.

"Should we check for supplies?" Jake asked, but Bill gestured for him to back away. A metallic stench rose from the ground.

Jake mumbled something and walked to the side of the tipi. Bill noticed him sway. He looked unglued in his pink hat.

"Oh shit." Jake's tone was just above a whisper.

"What?" Bill walked over to Jake and examined the poles that surrounded the tent.

Stakes, not poles. The blood glistened—fresh—as if the wood had been doused a few hours ago.

"Whatcha doing there?" A man materialized from the shrubbery. He had a white beard, and wore a red-stained shirt paired with camouflage pants.

Bill saw Jake inch closer to where Bill stood.

"We don't want no trouble," Bill responded, one hand on his gun, the other on the rim of his hat.

"They, all of them, want trouble," the man declared and moved forward.

Bill stood his ground and changed his speech, hoping to better relate to the bearded man. "Let us go in peace and we say nothin' about you, we don't need nothin' from you."

"No one ever needs anything." The man leaped at Bill, knocking him over, the gun falling from his hand. Then the old man jumped on top of him and punched Bill. "You son-ofa—"

Before the man could finish his sentence, Bill cracked him in the jaw, knocking out a tooth. A streak of blood colored the bearded man's face from his mouth to his ear. Bill pushed the old man off and hurried to get his gun, but the old man kicked it away. Jake ran at the old man, but the old man slugged him in the gut and Jake went down. The old man scrambled to his tipi. *This can't be good.*

Bill saw Jake regain his strength and fish for something in his pocket. He heard a continued mumbling coming from Jake's direction. Bill grabbed his hunting knife raising it in preparation. The old man reappeared with an ax and flailed toward Jake, but not before Bill tripped him. The ax flew out of his hands and stuck in one of the wooden stakes, cracking it down the middle. From lying on his back, the old man flipped to standing, and he waved his fists at Bill and Jake.

"You gonna kill me naw? You gonna kill me?" He jumped from side to side like a boxer and then stopped and titled his head.

"Like I said, we don't want any trouble." Bill kept his stance, knife in hand, ready to strike.

"Feck you." The old man launched at Bill, who sidestepped, swirled and kicked the old man in the butt.

"I won't hesitate to use my knife next time," Bill warned and his knuckles turned white on the knife-bearing hand.

"No he won't! Aaaah!" Jake screamed and ran towards the old man, toppled over a branch and somersaulted nearly hitting one of the stakes. A moment passed and then Jake burst out laughing and began to roll around on the ground.

The old man stared at him and then started to giggle himself.

"You guys aren't bounty hunters. You can barely stand on your feet." He looked at Jake and let out another chuckle shaking his head. "Here, come in."

Bill didn't move.

"You look like you're in need of a recuperation. Especially the one over there fumbling with the pink hat." He snorted.

Bill looked over at Jake, and then back at the old man, weighing his options.

"Come on. I have water." The old man bowed, opening the flap to his tipi.

August 2060 – Present Day
Jake Deen – The Red Rocks
Road to Livingsworth, Nevada

"Oh the Red Rocks, what a piece of shit, eh?" The old man, Pike Turner, sat on a plush rainbow pillow across from Bill and Jake in the tipi. It smelled of suede, and feathered dream catchers of all sizes hung from the top. The air inside was cool. It felt refreshing.

Pike had given them water, but now they moved on to his homemade wine. He cultivated his own special dirt, which allowed him to grow grapevines in the dry, hot weather. The wine seemed to have a stunning effect on the old man—he wouldn't stop talking. Jake, now semi-hydrated and his hand re-wrapped with the old man's special balsam and cloth, quieted down.

"You know what they call me here? The goddam bandit decapitator." The man chugged from his wooden cup and red drops settled in his white beard.

Jake's eyes widened. "You're him?" Jake sipped on the wine like a child suckling at its mother's breast. A familiar warmth filled his belly.

"I guess you could say that. Hell, you can say whatever, everyone else does. I kinda like it, 'xcept the feckin' bounty hunters. One or two each month, gotta run 'em off as usual. That's why I have the stakes outside. Nothing on there but grape juice, or if I get some, animal blood. Got lucky with me brains though and this special dirt. Now I make wine like the gods."

Nuthouse gods maybe.

"If the damn government gave a shit about this place and got some real police, there wouldn't need to be no feckin' hunters. Feckin' leeches."

Bill sat quietly, his dark eyes and face like stone.

Pike swayed as he sat there on his fluffy pillow and continued, "This place has turned me into something else. I was going crazy out there with the ads, moved to the Red Rocks. Thought I'd get better. But now look at me! Alone, fighting off the rest of the world who believe I'm a killer who takes people's heads off!"

Jake suppressed a laugh, and then asked, "Have you been here a long time?"

"Right after 8/6/2040, around 2042, I came here, when they had just moved everyone. I remember the train ride here and the step I took through the invisible barrier the government told me about. I had all me gear, me music player, me phone, me tablet. I thought I'd walk through and boom! Everything would turn off. But what happened? Nothin'. Just nowhere to plug it in to recharge and no service. I kept everything until the batteries died. Buried it all in my personal altar a mile off. Sometimes I go visit to check if somehow they'll magically turn on."

Jake tried to remember when he had gotten to the Red Rocks. Had he brought stuff with him too, or had his father confiscated everything? A fog surrounded the memory and he silenced his mind, putting his attention back on Pike.

"And then there was that time a woman—a butt naked woman—ran in here and—"

"Listen, Pike," Bill said, "we appreciate your company, but we need to be heading out." Pike's face fell and he put his head down.

"It's not anything to do with you, we just need to get going," Jake chimed in. He looked at Bill when Pike still hadn't lifted his head. Jake nudged the old man.

Snore.

"Is he asleep?" Jake mouthed and let out a laugh. Bill started to get up. Jake moved over the man and went for the wine container, but Bill shook his head. "Why not?" asked Jake. "He doesn't need it anymore." A louder snore erupted from Pike's nose.

"No," Bill said, and they left.

~ ~ ~

That night Bill and Jake sat by the campfire, close to the flames. They had settled near the parched river bed on the side of a hill, which guarded them from the bone-chilling wind. The moonless night offered no heat; instead, little droplets fell from the heavy sky, bringing out the earthy scent of wet rock and sagebrush.

"Any plans for when we get to Livingsworth?" Bill asked.

"No. I'm just going to be glad to be back in a nice bed and take a bath," Jake said, trying to tackle his dreaded hair with a rubber band. His hand throbbed from the spider bite.

"Yes, that will be nice. But then it's back on the road." Bill looked off into the distance, the fire reflecting in his dark eyes.

"Looks like you're on the road a lot. What do you do there . . . here . . . in the Red Rocks?" Jake asked. He saw Bill's right eyebrow jump.

"I'd tell you, but I'd have to kill you," Bill said, his voice low.

Jake laughed, but Bill didn't smile. He took a sip of water. They sat in silence.

Jake heard a shuffle in the bushes about twenty feet away, and Bill perked up putting his finger to his lips. Jake searched the perimeter until he found three pairs of floating eyes glowing in the dark. He strained his neck trying to find the bodies they belong to, but couldn't.

Bill picked up the water canteen and a bag of dried meat. "Stay here," he said. Jake nodded, but as soon as Bill was six feet away he got up and followed him. Jake's eyes adjusted to the darkness, and he made out three large shapes with upward curved tusks which shone white when the light from the fire hit them at the right angle. Boars, Jake thought. He crept forward and squatted behind a shrub when he was close enough to see Bill's movements.

He saw Bill slow his pace as he got closer to the animals, then watched him hold out his hand toward the ferals. The boar in the middle let out a squeal and charged towards Bill. The other two followed. Bill jumped off to the side disappearing in the greenery.

Jake's gaze followed the boars nervously as they ran towards Bill, husks ready. Grunts and squeals pierced the air, accompanying the stampede of the run. Jake ran back to the fire and then—

Bang! Squeal! Grunt!

Jake couldn't catch his breath and the pain in his hand escalated from a nagging pulse to an angry ache. He fished out a small bottle of wine from his boot which he took from Pike's tent despite Bill's protest, and sipped it.

"You okay?"

Jake jumped, not hearing Bill come up behind him. He then put his arm over the bottle in an attempt to hide it from Bill's view.

"You don't need to do that," Bill said. "I know you took the wine."

Jake made an innocent face and offered the bottle to Bill. Bill accepted and swallowed almost a third of what was left.

Jake raised his eyebrows and looked away, patting his hands on his jeans. "What were you trying to do back there?" Jake shifted so he could take the bottle out of Bill's hand.

"The daytime heat is not a friend to these animals. I was trying to get close enough to see if they were tagged. If they were and wandered off not far away from here, it could be a worthwhile trip to bring them back to their owner. They'd be back to safety, and we'd get a refill on water, and possibly a meal."

"You risked your life for water and a meal?" Jake asked and thought he saw a half-smile flash over Bill's face and disappear.

"This isn't my first time dealing with boars," Bill said.

Interesting, Jake thought, although he wasn't surprised. "Do you do this sort of thing for a living?"

Bill lifted tobacco leaf from his pouch and rubbed it between his fingers. He didn't respond.

"I do odd jobs wherever I am. You know, help out here and there," Jake offered.

"Like what?" Bill lit his rolled cigarette.

"Like bartending, or construction, or whatever jobs I can find. It doesn't matter to me, as long as they pay."

Bill nodded. "And that's all you've done since you arrived at the Red Rocks?"

"You don't need much in the Red Rocks. Plus, it makes life easier. No commitments."

"You do have one commitment," Bill said. He looked at the bottle Jake was holding.

"Yes." Jake sighed and looked off to the side. A clap of thunder roared in the distance.

"I've been down that path as well," Bill said, pain lurking in his voice.

"And now?"

"And now I have a drink time and again, but I don't need to get drunk to make it through the day." Bill took a long drag and then put his cigarette out.

Jake finished chewing the rest of his dried meat.

"May I ask what made you go down this path in the first place?"

"My father—he fell to the bottle after my mom left. I learned from him when I was really young. There was a point where I thought about quitting, back in the Metropolitans, I didn't want to end up like him. But then, he sent me away here, just sent me away to fend for myself."

Shuddering, Jake pulled his sweater closer around him, he was glad he came across it in the deserted tent. It was checkered with faded squares where the Metropolitan ads used to be.

"That's a long time—you said you were here, what, fifteen years?"

"Yeah, just about." Jake fumbled with the rolling papers.

"I held on to my habit for about seven years; it wasn't easy to break free, but I did it," Bill said and put on his hat to keep his hair down as the wind picked up.

They sat in silence, smoking.

Jake noticed Bill sliding a ring on and off of his finger. "Is that why you started?"

Bill nodded.

"Did she leave you or something?" Jake asked, thinking about his own mother, and how she left when he was young.

"Or something . . ."

Jake handed the bottle over to Bill and lit up. They listened to the crickets sing their nighttime symphony.

August 2060 – Present Day
Bill Vos – The Red Rocks
Livingsworth, Nevada

Two days later, Bill and Jake arrived in Livingsworth as the sun was starting to set. They walked toward the city center, observing all the dusty people in the dusty town. A mix of red and brown, of wood and brick, peppered the sides of the main road. Stands filled with fresh fruit and vegetables were tended by sweat-drenched vendors. Couples walked hand in hand, excited for their terrace dinners. Beggars, ignored by the public eye, stood in alleyways trying to make their presence known. The smell of horses thickened the air.

Jake and Bill stopped at the first hotel they saw. It had a cinder block exterior, and cool, damp air made its way to Bill and Jake each time the door opened.

"We're here," Bill confirmed.

"So, what do I owe you?" Jake started rummaging through his pant pockets.

Bill waved him off.

"I appreciate it," Jake said. "Would you by any chance need any help on your next trip? You did say you'd be back on the road again soon."

Bill looked up. "I'm not looking for help at this time."

"It's always better to ride with two people, right?"

Bill shook his head. "I don't think it would be a good idea."

"Bill, look. I'm neat, I ride well, I learn fast. One could say I have Red Rocks in my blood." Jake straightened his posture.

"Jake, as you might have guessed, I make deliveries for a living. I have a set schedule. I cannot miss my dates."

"That's okay. I will make all of the dates."

"You have a drinking problem. This makes you a liability. I can't trust a guy to be vigilant on the road when he's seeing double."

"I'll stop drinking."

Bill squinted his eyes.

"Okay. I won't drink when we are on the road."

There *are* times when I have to decline runs because the orders are too large. I can use an extra man, Bill thought.

"How about you take me along for the next ride. If it doesn't work out, you don't have to pay me."

He did learn quick, and wasn't a nuisance. At least not when he was hydrated.

"Fine," Bill said. "You'll need to find yourself a horse."

"No bikes?"

He should know better than to ask that. Bill thought for a moment about rescinding his offer, but something in his gut told him to give Jake a shot. "Normal bikes can't carry much. Motor bikes are too noisy and gas is too expensive and hard to come by."

Jake nodded. "Okay, horse it is. When do we meet and where?"

"Here, take this." Bill dug out from his jacket a piece of paper and a pen, and he scribbled down a name and address. "I have an associate here in Livingsworth. I'll be back here in two weeks. If you want to ride with me, leave a message with him."

Jake took the paper. "Out of curiosity, how much money does one ride bring in?"

"Enough for a decent place to stay, food, and spending money for a month in a town like this."

Jake coughed.

Bill paid attention to the tremor in Jake's hand as he reached to shake it. He knew he was taking a chance on the kid and remembered the time someone had given him one.

October 2050 ~ 10 Years Ago
Bill Vos – Metropolitans
San Francisco, California

"I'm glad you came to us and not your current employer. They would've put you in a box as soon as you asked to get out, you know." The silver-haired man spoke with an Eastern European accent. "Of course we could too." He gestured at Bill with his gun. "But I have good feeling about you." He grinned, showing several gold teeth. "And when I have good feeling, I take chance."

They sat in a small underground office. The man across from him in a kinetic mesh chair that no doubt cost thousands of dollars. Bill himself sat on a black metal stool, which operated as a metal scanner. The table between them had a computer screen embedded in the top, it received a signal from the stool, and highlighted in neon green the weapon placements on Bill's body. In the corner of the room, a plastic crate full of multicolored wires blinked with red, green, and yellow lights. It was an ad blocker; Bill had used them many times.

"Can you get me everything I need?" Bill asked, his gaze following the gun held by nicotine-stained fingers.

"As long as your intel checks out, you'll get everything you need for a fresh start. The world, as they say, is your oyster." The man leaned over the desk, his breath smelled of vodka and decay.

"It will," Bill confirmed. "What do I need to do next?" He watched the silver-haired man's every movement, and kept his hand on the combat knife wrapped in a band against his thigh.

"Next, you get used to your new name: Bill Vos. I thought it had a ring to it." The man coughed and laughed.

"Bill Vos," Bill repeated. "And now what?"

"And now you wait."

August 2060 – Present Day
Jake Deen – The Red Rocks
Livingsworth, Nevada

Jake watched Bill go, walking tall, leading his dark as night horse by the reins. Then Jake caught a glimpse of himself in the tarnished hotel window. He looked like hell. He sniffed his hoodie and gagged. *I need to get cleaned up*, he thought.

He checked into the hotel with the crumpled bills he pulled out of his boot. He asked for a bath, and the hotel manager brought him six pails of hot water to pour into the aluminum tub. As soon as he got in, the water, now only lukewarm, turned brown. *Disgusting.* He laughed at himself and scrubbed the grime off with homemade glycerin soap. Afterward, he'd check out the hotel bar. He looked over at the tiny wad of bills on the night table. *Maybe.*

He got out of the bath, toweled off with a dirty piece of linen, and put on a fresh pair of jeans and a black T-shirt—perks of a hotel in a large town. His travel clothes needed to be tossed.

Jake looked at himself in the cracked mirror above the basin. Eyes tired, nose bruised, lips cracked. The giant dread of blond hair fell down to his shoulders. He tried to brush it out, but was only half successful. He left the two-day stubble—it suited his traveled look. Still got it, he thought as he flexed his right arm in the mirror and then coughed up a rough piece of lung butter.

Jake wondered if this was all a sign. If he can make it to the meeting with Bill, then he can make some money, find a woman, build a house. He could move away from his life of being thrown from one place to the next. He could start a new life—a better one.

He imagined a cottage on the outskirts of town, a covered porch and two padded lawn chairs facing the horizon. A woman in a long pale gown standing next to him while he sits there, her hand on his shoulder, hair blowing in the wind. She looks down at him and smiles, and he at her.

August 2060 – Present Day
Bill Vos – The Red Rocks
Kingman, Nevada

Bill took off his hat and pushed two packages across a wooden table to the bald, corpulent man dressed in an expensive Italian suit.

"Here you go, Tommy," he said, his deep voice muted in the soundproof room.

"You made it to Kingman quicker than expected," Tommy commented, weighing the packages in his hands.

"I made good time," Bill said, sliding his fingers across his thick eyebrows.

Bill disliked Kingman, a small town north of Livingsworth, composed of several mansions, a bar, and an escort house, and occupied by rich, dishonest men—like the one in front of him.

Tommy examined the wax seals on the packages, then put on his glasses and took a closer look to make sure none were cracked or broken.

"Looks good," he said, and walked to the safe in the corner of the room.

"I need to ask you to send—"

"Yes, yes, I know, money to the Metropolitans." Tommy counted out two piles of Red Rock notes. Bill hated that this dirty man was the messenger between him and the last family he had.

"Same account?" Tommy asked, waiting to make a note in his ledger.

Bill nodded.

"Here you go." Tommy handed Bill one of the stacks of cash with a sweaty hand.

"Is there a new run schedule?" Bill asked, placing the money inside his jean jacket.

Tommy took out a white envelope from the drawer.

"I can run double the amount this time," Bill said.

Tommy raised an eyebrow. "You sure?"

Bill gave a nod and Tommy took out a second envelope. "All the pick-up/drop-off locations and delivery dates are in there per usual."

Bill took both and stood up, towering over the short greasy man.

"Always a pleasure, Bill." Tommy opened the door.

Bill gave a somber look and walked out.

August 2060 – Present Day
Jake Deen – The Red Rocks
Livingsworth, Nevada

Clean, dread-free, and determined, Jake walked around Livingsworth looking for the street that Bill wrote down for him. It was the day after Bill had dropped him off and he was on a mission.

Roosters crowed and early risers bustled, prepping for the day ahead. The light breeze brought no relief to the already fiery heat. Jake walked by a bar and restaurant where a young man with a mustache wiped the dirt bespattered windows and wrote today's specials on the glass: pork and cabbage stew, pork and cabbage tacos, roasted pork with a side of boiled cabbage. *That's Red Rocks variety for you.*

Jake passed a man with skin like the leather vest he wore. He was brushing his rust-colored horse. Several tubes stuck out of the large saddlebag the horse carried. A messenger, Jake guessed.

As he walked to the town center, three girls in their early twenties walked by him, their knee-length skirts and revealing tops wrinkled, their make-up smeared. The wind picked up and the girls held down their skirts, but one was too late, and everyone on the street got a peek of her knickers. Jake laughed to himself.

He walked farther and his mouth watered as the smell of sausage and roasted corn wafted by. He wished he hadn't spent most of his money on booze the night before. He stopped in the middle of the street and watched a vendor in a tie-dye shirt and jeans prep each piece of meat and corn with care, rationing out the exact amount of salt and sugar to cover each kernel. *I wonder how much—Oomph!* Someone bumped into his shoulder.

"Excuse me," said a woman's voice.

Damn it, what a b—Jake looked up. A woman was standing in front of him, her slight smile drew him in—highlighted lips bright, against pale skin, glacier eyes—hypnotic.

Jake realized his stare was intrusive, when she took a small step back. "I'm so sorry," she said, and bent down to pick up a few items that had fallen out of her purse.

"Let me help you." Jake crouched on the sidewalk next to her; she smelled of strawberries.

"Thank you," she said, after they'd gathered everything.

Jake watched her walk away. He stood for a minute before realizing he was making a fist. When he opened it, he saw several business cards and a twenty note inside. Old habits, he sighed, annoyed with himself. But at least now he could get something to eat.

August 2060 – Present Day
Jake Deen – The Red Rocks
Livingsworth, Nevada

"Excuse me, sir," Jake asked a man indulging in tobacco outside a small wooden door.

"Yes?" the skinny, short man with watery eyes responded. He had a thin curved mustache and protruding eyes. He reminded Jake of a circus performer.

"Is this Bobby's, by any chance?" Jake asked.

"Certainly is! The friendliest place you'll find in the city!" The old man gave a high-pitched laugh and gestured for Jake to come in.

It had taken him three hours to find the bar, which was on a hidden side street on the opposite side of town from

Jake's hotel. On the side of it was a gate that led to the stables where one could park their horse. It looked full.

He went inside and walked around. The bar was a lot bigger than it looked from the outside. He calculated it to fit close to sixty people. Jake observed the decor and nodded in approval; he could tell it wasn't cheap. Artisan stools accented the lengthy bar which could fit a dozen people. Bottles of whiskey and sweet wine filled the shelves behind it. Above the shelves, hung a sword with a black and red handle. Chessboards sat out with half-finished games on all of the tables; one board sat on the bar with sticky note that read: *your move.* Gas lights lined the walls and a large chandelier hung in the middle of the ceiling. The place smelled of homemade food and wood fire.

Jake sat down at the bar, listening to the light sound of acoustic guitar coming from a gramophone near the register. The bartender was serving whiskey to a young, tattooed man to his right.

Jake caught the bartender's eye after he was finished topping off the pour. "Are you Bobby?"

"I am. Who's asking?" He looked at Jake over his glasses. He was of medium height and build, and although his Japanese roots painted a young face, the strands of gray hair told a different story. He wore a button up shirt with jeans and there was an ease to his movements and a twinkle in his eyes.

"A guy named Bill told me about your place," Jake said, and shifted in his seat. A few of the men around the bar turned to look at Jake.

Bobby's face showed a hint of surprise. "Bill?"

"He didn't give me a last name, but he's tall, cowboy hat, bandana?" Jake gestured with each word. "He gave me this." Jake handed Bobby the note.

Bobby looked closely at the bottom right-hand corner. There was a tiny raised stamp that Jake hadn't noticed earlier. Bobby ran his finger over the stamp and his face softened.

"Now, what can I do you for?"

"I'll be frank with you, Bobby. I'm looking to make a few notes for a horse and a place to stay. I'm riding out with Bill in two weeks." Jake clasped his hands together and leaned over the bar to get Bobby's full attention.

"I'll be frank with you too—what's your name?"

"Jake."

"I'll be frank with you too, Jake. I don't have anything available right now. It's been a slow month and I can't afford to pay out cash." Bobby gave him an apologetic look and took out a rag to wipe down the counter.

Jake's shoulders slumped. *Shit.* He tapped his fingers on the table.

"I noticed a part of your wooden floor needs to be repaired." Jake pointed at a loose board in the back of the bar. "What if I work on that in exchange for a place to stay?"

"I don't have any rooms I can give up. The ones I have are filled with long-term tenants." Bobby looked off to the side and smoothed out his neatly trimmed mustache which was complemented by a short goatee.

"Okay, what if I sleep on the pile of hay in the stable and take care of the horses?" Jake persisted. "Then when it's time to ride, you let me borrow a horse. When I get back, I'll return your horse and give you enough notes to cover renting the animal for the trip."

"And if you come back without my horse?" Bobby gave him a pointed look.

"Then I will pay the full amount for it."

"I want to help, but like I said, I can't afford to be charitable right now." Bobby took out a bottle of whiskey and poured a shot to the man who sat down next to Jake. The man took it and walked to the back of the bar after waving to a young woman. Jake's mouth watered and he took the dirty shot glass, grabbed the uncorked bottle, and poured himself a round. He appreciated the nutty, smoky liquor. It made him feel more like himself.

"Did you just pour yourself *my* whiskey?" Bobby said, appalled.

"I'll pay for it." Jake reached into his pocket to take out the last of his notes.

"You don't do that in my place," Bobby said. "Get the fuck out."

"I didn't mean to, I—"

"There is no excuse for that. Get out," Bobby said.

Shit! Jake thought. I can't start off like this.

"I'm going to count to three before you get your disrespectful ass out of here."

Jake glanced around, trying to figure out something he could do or say to convince Bobby not to kick him out; his eyes landed on the chessboard with the note that read: *your move*.

"What if I play you for it?" Jake asked. Two of the men in the bar moved closer, a curious spark in their eyes.

Bobby looked directly at him, his dark eyes glittered with amusement, but then he started to count. "One."

"Hear me out. If I lose I will leave the bar."

Bobby didn't budge. "Two."

"I will leave the bar and never come back."

Bobby looked intrigued. "And if you win?"

Got him! Jake smiled.

"If I win, I get a place to stay, a horse, and a small amount of spending money. All as a loan." Jake counted off the requirements on his fingers. "All to be repaid when I come back from the ride. In addition, I'll also fix the flooring for you at no charge."

Bobby smoothed out his mustache. "How about if I win, you never come back to Livingsworth." Bobby poured himself a shot and drank it. "And if I lose, I will give you what you asked for, but, you'll owe me double what I lend you."

Jake laughed and shook his head.

"Well?" Bobby asked.

Jake reached out his hand.

August 2060 – Present Day
Jake Deen – The Red Rocks
Livingsworth, Nevada

"Ten, nine, eight, seven..." A crowd had gathered around the wooden table where Jake and Bobby made their moves to an analog chess timer with a mechanical windup clock and a black plastic case. Five men encircled them, four behind Bobby and one behind Jake, chanting as the timer clicked down. They had each placed a small bet.

It was game three out of three. Jake had lost the first and convinced Bobby to play for two out of three. Bobby had lost the second, and the current game was the tie-breaker.

All eyes were on Bobby, his forehead creased and his mouth held a tight line.

Bobby moved his queen and hit the round button on the timer. "Check," he said, and the three men behind him erupted in cheer. "Go Bobby!" The tattooed man slapped him on the shoulder.

Jake ran his fingers over the sleek marble of the pieces he had conquered. If he lost, he'd lose his chance to ride with Bill. Lose his chance to make some real money. Lose his chance at a different life. He concentrated on his next move, but the persistent timer made it difficult. Each tick and tock was grating away at his nerves one by one. Each second taking hope of a fresh start farther and farther away. If he lost, he'd be back to his drifter life with yet another town added to his list of towns he'd never come back to. The list grew bigger each month as pissed off bar owners and boyfriends posed threats to his wellbeing.

Heart pounding and palms wet, he moved his king one square to the right, taking him out of harm's way. *Click*. He pressed the button with satisfaction.

Bobby frowned. He wiped his hands on his button up shirt and followed the king with his queen. "Check."

Fuck. Jake maneuvered away from the queen once more, setting his king in a position where if Bobby were to pursue, he'd lose his own queen.

Click.

Jake's breath caught in his throat as he saw his opportunity. "Check!" he said, moving his bishop diagonally in line with Bobby's king. Everybody held their breath, waiting for Bobby to make his next move. The tension was taut as a tightrope.

"Damn it!" Bobby said and slammed his hand against the table, knocking over a rook and knight; they rolled off the board in surrender. He put the pieces upright and moved a random pawn, defeated.

"Checkmate!" Jake yelled and looked up to find that behind the men who had placed bets, the whole bar was watching. A mix of men and women, a mix of young and old—everybody roared. The four men behind Bobby each threw down a stack of Red Rock notes on the table.

"The underdog wins! Looks like it was a good day to take a chance," the burly man sitting behind Jake cried out in delight as he grabbed a Red Rock note out of the tattooed man's hand across from him.

After a moment of being silent, Bobby stood up and shook Jake's hand.

"Three out of five?" Jake offered.

"No. It's good to finally meet a worthy opponent."

September 2060 – Present Day
Bill Vos – The Red Rocks
Wells, Nevada

Three days after meeting with Tommy, Bill arrived in Wells, a small town near the Utah border. Wells was a sad town, populated with abandoned structures each day struggling to stay upright. His plan was to spend his time resting and mapping out his next ride. He had no time to see or talk to anyone, nor the desire. He sat in his house, which mirrored the brick ones down the street, but his had no entrance. The only way in was a passage from the bar next door, which never opened. His bed, in the corner, was the only piece of furniture except for the two floor-to-ceiling shelves, which housed hundreds of books. A lonely guitar, the only decoration, leaned against the back wall. He hasn't played it in years.

From underneath the box spring he pulled a small, black safe. He opened it with care, and took out a photograph, its corners curled and ink blurred. Staring back at him was an honest smile, roused from happiness and joy. It was the moment after they had said their vows—she looked angelic in her tiara—a halo on a fated soul.

I wish you were here. He placed the photo on his pillow, opened up his half-finished *The Three Musketeers*, her favorite book, and began to read.

September 2060 – Present Day
Jake Deen – The Red Rocks
Livingsworth, Nevada

Jake stood in the room that Bobby had given him; it was a storage room, but they had cleared it out and brought in a cot. He stared into a foggy mirror above a basin filled with water, as he moved the straight razor down his cheek, cutting away budding blond hairs. He admired himself: his face fresh, his muscles pronounced. Most of his bruises, from being left in the desert, had faded.

He went over to put on a clean black shirt, and saw something fall on the ground—a pink business card with a hummingbird on the front, a name and address on the back. It took him a second to remember the girl that smelled like strawberries. "Anna Faroe," he mouthed.

He flipped the card over several times and thumbed the raised font as he sat down on his bed. Then he pulled out a bottle of whiskey from underneath and took a swallow. He looked at the card again. Another swallow. Should he return the cards to her? he wondered. A sip. It would be a good deed. Another sip. Would it be weird, though? A swig.

~ ~ ~

Hours later, the warm afternoon air caressed Jake's skin as he walked through the town down the now familiar streets in search of the woman. Soon after, he was knocking on the door of a pale yellow single family home with a white porch, and a small backyard he could see over the gate.

He looked down at his dirty shirt and knee-torn jeans tucked into his worn-out work boots. Anxiety began to sneak through his drunk confidence. He wanted to leave.

The door swung open and there she stood, eyes the color of sky reflected in sunlight. "Hello," she said.

"Hello," Jake answered. She looked stunning in a pale periwinkle, kimono robe; little hummingbirds danced on it as she moved.

"May I help you?"

"Um . . . I . . . um . . ." Jake dug the cards out from his pocket. "You dropped these when you ran into me—about five days ago? I thought I'd return them to you. They looked expensive." He shifted from his toes to his heels.

"Thank you." She took the cards and started closing the door.

"Wait." Jake put his foot into the doorway.

"Excuse me," Anna said, crossing her arms over her chest.

"Is everything okay out there?" a coarse woman's voice called from inside the house.

"I'll be right in," Anna called back. "I have to go," she said and turned away.

Jake pulled his foot back, but not enough to let the door close. "Would you like to get coffee sometime?"

"I can't." Anna was looking him over.

"Can't or won't?" Jake asked, knowing he was being too forward.

"Does it make a difference?" She held his gaze, making him uncomfortable, but eager.

"No," he said.

"Then goodbye." She moved the door to close it, and her kimono billowed open, exposing the swell of her breast. His eyes widened. "How can I change your mind?"

"You can't," she said and closed the door, but he stuck his hand in right before she could, and it got pinched. He sucked his breath in through his teeth, but held his hand in place.

"I came all this way. Can't you just give me a chance?"

"You're being impolite," Anna said sternly.

"Who is it?" the voice from inside the house echoed.

"No one," Anna responded. "I'll be right there."

"I'll leave right now if you agree to go on a date with me."

Anna laughed, eyes shining, and shook her head. "Fine. If I do, you promise to leave now?"

Jake smiled and nodded.

"Come over tomorrow at seven."

~ ~ ~

On the way back to his hotel, Jake crossed through the Livingsworth Town Square which consisted of a brick police and fire station, the city hall office, and the government supply store—Red Rocks Stock. Deciding he should get Anna something, Jake went into the musty shop. It was lined with aisles of half-filled shelves of beans, rice, toilet paper, soap, toothpaste, matches. Dust had collected on the shelves where batteries, medicine, and tobacco were supposed to be. A trading table stood in the back with candles, cards, porcelain statuettes, and other knickknacks people brought in to exchange for other goods.

"Do you have any chocolate?" Jake asked the thin, pointy-nosed man behind the counter. He reminded Jake of a bird.

"It's not cheap. Twenty-five notes."

The number made Jake stagger backward—he could get a one night's stay in a low-end hotel for that amount. "Nothing cheaper?" he asked.

The man shook his head. "Not until the next supply drop."

Jake slumped his shoulders and walked once more from one side of the shop to the other, then hovered around the trading table, browsing the offerings until his eye stopped on a tiny hummingbird statuette—Anna's robe had hummingbirds on it.

"Thank you," Jake said, waving to the store clerk.

"Sorry you couldn't find anything. Things tend sell out quickly here. The best stuff is gone in the first week after a drop."

Jake gave a nod. Outside, he lit a rolled cigarette and took out the statuette from his pocket.

September 2060 – Present Day
Anna Faroe – The Red Rocks
Livingsworth, Nevada

Anna stood in front of the mirror, adjusting her navy blue dress. It was cut in the middle down to her waist, her breasts flowed freely underneath. She thought about the night ahead and fluffed her raven hair, giving it volume to sit just above her mid back. *Knock. Knock.* Anna sprayed lilac perfume and walked to the door. Jake stood there staring, no words leaving his lips. My little blue dress always works like a charm, she thought.

"Nice to see you again." She held out her manicured hand. Jake kissed it, and, as he bent down, a loose strand of his hair tickled her skin. She led him in, admiring his tidy jeans, clean shave, and pulled back hair. A nice change from yesterday, she noted.

"Nice place."

"Thank you." Anna loved her house: to her it meant growth, success—a place of healing. The cozy living room was accented with a vintage coffee table, couch, and violet walls. The cracked leather of the brown couch was covered with a hummingbird blanket. Scented candles sprinkled throughout the room danced to the breeze coming in from the window. They smelled of spring.

"What's your name?" She motioned for him to sit.

"Jake," he said, his jade eyes bright. She could tell he was a tad nervous.

"Would you like something to drink?" Anna asked, her voice was velvety, inviting. "Wait, don't tell me." She walked to the oak liquor cabinet across the room. Recalling his whiskey breath, she poured him two fingers.

"How did you know?" Jake wiped a hand on his jeans.

"I just do." Anna smiled and walked back to her bar.

She looked at the three bottles of wine left; she selected a dark red, poured herself a glass, and settled next to Jake on the couch.

"Cheers." Anna lifted her glass.

"Cheers." Jake mirrored her. They both took a sip and sat in silence.

"So . . . what brought you over to the Red Rocks?" Jake managed meekly.

"My free spirit." She shook her head back and forth and her hair followed—a dark sea of silky waves.

"Did you live the whole time in Livingsworth?" Jake took a calculated swallow.

"Yes. All five years. And you?"

"I've traveled around since getting here. I've been here a long time, about fifteen years."

"What brought you here?"

"It's a long story," he said, sadness underlining his tone.

There was a pause. Anna looked at Jake, her stare boring into him, circling his deepest secrets. *Unpleasant past, but to what extent?* She liked peeling emotional layers, opening up the rawness, and remedying each one.

He looked away and shifted in his seat. "So, why *did* you come to the Red Rocks?"

"Guess!" Anna clasped her hands together and tilted her head to the side.

Jake looked around the room once more, then he stood up and walked over to a redwood bookshelf behind the couch to examine its contents. After a minute, he walked back and said, "It seems to me that you were a dedicated student, but the superficial tech-based world was not rewarding spiritually. So, you finished your studies, and moved to the simple life of the Red Rocks where you could pursue your art and journey of the inner self."

Anna laughed. "Don't believe everything you see." She nudged him playfully on the shoulder and saw him relax.

"Well then, where did I get it wrong?"

"I never said you did." She smiled coyly.

"Well then, what was it that you studied?"

"History," she said, "focused on the rise of technology." Anna fingered the hem of her skirt. "How about yourself? Did you study anything?"

"I never made it that far in school, I came here before I could start college."

"Well, I'm sure you've learned a lot in the Red Rocks." Anna took his glass and went to refill it.

"Yes, a different set of life lessons," he said, and the light dimmed as a candle went out. "So what do you do now?"

"I offer companionship." Anna watched Jake's expression transform from curiosity to judgment, a moist layer forming on his brow.

"Um, what does that mean?" Jake brought his hand up to his chin.

"It means people hire me to spend time with them." Her tone was soft, yet clear.

"So you're a prostitute." He sighed, his emerald eyes harboring disappointment.

"No." Anna gave him a pointed look.

"Then what?"

She walked over and sat on the arm of the couch. "I meet with people to talk, to offer friendship and healing—companionship."

"And sex." His voice spiked a level.

"Sometimes." Anna looked off to the right, her feathery eyelashes catching the dim light and capturing a painted bird on the wall in a shadow cage.

Jake reached into his faded ad-checkered sweater pocket to make sure he had his cash so he could pay her. "Why did you wait to tell me?"

"I thought you knew. You had my card." She put her hands in her lap.

Jake looked away.

She said, "I don't take just any clients. I meet with them to see if there is a connection—mentally, physically, or on a rare occasion, both."

"What do you think about me?"

"I can tell which type of company you came here for."

"Oh yeah?"

"You told yourself you're here to have a conversation, to find someone, but what you really want"—Anna moved closer to Jake, her dress sliding up—"is this." She placed his hand on her thigh. "Yes?" she asked and could tell he felt her heat as his face flushed and heart beat quickened.

September 2060 – Present Day
Jake Deen – The Red Rocks
Livingsworth, Nevada

Jake and Anna lay entangled on the floor, breathing heavily. The room was now completely dark and saturated with the scent of sex and sweat. Anna giggled as Jake traced his finger along the ink lines on her chest, where a small blue and purple hummingbird lived.

"Why hummingbirds?" he asked.

"They always fascinated me. They work so hard, beat their wings so fast. They live hovering from moment to moment, house to house, leaving smiling faces behind. They are the bird that everyone wants, but that no one has the heart to take captive. They are too beautiful to keep in a cage."

"I see." Jake leaned in and Anna lifted her head for a kiss. "Would this hummingbird let me keep her attention a little bit longer?"

Anna laughed. "My fee is set for a night, so you can go or you can stay. But if you stay, you'll have to get me another glass of wine," she said with the mischievous smile.

Jake, still naked, poured another drink for each of them. "So how did you end up in this profession, if you don't mind me asking?" He handed her the drink, and Anna put a blanket down so they didn't have to sit on the cold floor. She laid on her stomach, her hair cascading down in a beautiful mess.

"I like to help people, I'm good at it," she reflected. "Good at listening, good at predicting what they want and when. It's not about sex with most clients, it's more about closeness—they need someone to talk to—to spend time with."

"Do you ever worry about getting attached?" Jake caressed the small of her back.

"No." She took a sip of wine. "I've learned how to compartmentalize my feelings."

"Are you someone else then, when you're working?"

"I pride myself on being very honest." She stared into his eyes and he felt his cheeks grow warm.

"What do you usually do then . . . with clients, if not . . . you know."

"A lot of time we simply talk—talk about their past, present, future . . . why they are alone."

"Do you give them advice?"

"Sometimes."

"Do they ever get angry or jealous?"

"Sometimes."

September 2060 – Present Day
Jake Deen – The Red Rocks
Livingsworth, Nevada

Jake left Anna's in the morning after a shared cup of coffee. It was the first time, in a long time, that he wished the woman he'd had sex with would be lying next to him the next day. The first time he didn't want to sneak out before she woke up. The first time he wasn't thrilled that there were no phones to call her back, or internet to get in touch. Most girls were insecure, most girls were needy, most girls were . . . boring. Not Anna.

He left the hummingbird statuette for her, hoping it would bring a smile to her face once she found it and remind her of him. He got back to his room refreshed. He changed his shirt, brushed out his tangled hair, then walked into the bar just as Bobby was opening the front door.

The place looked strange without people, musty and quiet. The first rays of sunshine were peeking through the windows and twinkling in the tear-dropped chandelier.

"How was your night?" Bobby asked, looking tired, hair unbrushed, shirt wrinkled.

"A gentleman never tells," Jake answered.

"Ha, you're no gentleman, Jake. Don't let anyone tell you different." They both laughed.

"You look like hell on the other hand," Jake noted.

"We had a busy night." Bobby gestured at the stack of unclean beer mugs in the back.

"That's good to hear."

"We haven't had a night like that in a long time," Bobby said as he took a rag and began wiping down the bar. Jake went over to help him.

"I'll be riding off with Bill soon," Jake said nonchalantly, while scrubbing old stew from the wood. "Have you known each other for a while?"

"He's a very private man," Bobby said, sidestepping the question.

"Does he work for himself?" Jake pushed on.

"It's not my place to say, but I know he does well for himself. You'll be able to pay me back in full after the ride."

"How about I pay you back right now. Let's play—all or nothing!" Jake joked.

"You're funny. How about I take you up on that after you get back from your trip? I'll have enough time to strategize and your brains will be wilted from the heat of desert."

This guy, Jake thought. "Bobby, really, thank you. I owe you."

"Everyone does," Bobby smiled.

September 2060 – Present Day
Bill Vos – The Red Rocks
Oasis, Nevada

Bill placed a bouquet onto the moss-covered stone in front of a geyser. It was created accidentally by a farmer who dug a well and discovered that the water inside was over two-hundred degrees. The nutrient-filled liquid had caused a colorful mineral growth to build up, shaping a beautiful fountain of nature.

Bill looked at the glimmering pinnacles protruding from the wet earth—they were majestic, kaleidoscopic, surreal. He loved this place, and he wished he could show it to the one person he loved the most. He had scattered some of her ashes here years ago. This spot brought Bill peace and comfort. Every time he saw the water shoot up, nurturing the life around, he felt her presence. *I promise that while I'm alive, I will take care of your family. Of everyone you loved. I miss you every day.*

September 2060 – Present Day
Anna Faroe – The Red Rocks
Livingsworth, Nevada

Anna smiled to herself, then walked out of her room and opened the door to meet a client named Sebastián Rousseau, a short, squat man with biceps the size of grapefruits. Long dark eyelashes lined his brown eyes, making them entrancing.

Anna has been seeing Sebastián for two years, working through the trauma of him losing his friends to the sickness that befell so many leading up to 8/6/2040.

"I've missed you," he said and took her into his arms. She kissed his neck and cheek.

"I've missed you too." She invited him in and they sat down. The candlelit room was alive with fiery shadows, and the smell of jasmine hung in the air.

"Do you want to start where we left off last time? You were telling me about your friend Maria, and how she wasn't able to walk down the streets."

Sebastián looked at Anna, and his eyes went to a place faraway, and then they fluttered shut. "She used to hit her head against the wall when she couldn't handle the noise and lights anymore."

Anna moved her hand up and down his leg in comfort.

"I don't know how many times I wished—"

Knock. Knock.

"Excuse me for one second," Anna said.

Knock. Knock. Knock. The second round of knocks came before she could get up. She knew who it was before she answered the door.

"Jake, now is not a good time," she said. He had come to her house every day for the last three days—every day since their first date. He showed up at random hours before and after work, hoping to catch her home. If she was busy, he would come back later.

"Anna, I need to see you. I want to see you now." Jake wrapped his arms around her and pulled her in for a kiss, pushing her inside the room.

Anna pulled away. "Jake, stop!"

"What the hell is this?" Sebastián exclaimed, and stood up.

"Another one?" Jake's cheeks reddened. "How many does that make?!"

"Jake, this is not a good time. You need to leave."

"I think you better listen to the lady and go."

"You." He pointed at Sebastián. "Don't speak to me. Never. Speak. To. Me." He stomped on the wooden floor, causing the wine glasses on her table to shake.

"You need to watch your mouth." Sebastián took a step toward Jake.

"Stop! Jake please go!" Anna stood between the two men, who were both breathing heavily. Sebastián's hands balled into fists and he was puffing his chest as he inched closer.

"Jake, you need to leave. Now!" Anna placed a hand on Sebastián's shoulder, signaling him to stop.

Jake looked at her, upset. "But Anna, I—"

"I said now, Jake. I will visit with you at a later time."

Jake's face fell and he walked out.

This boy is trouble, Anna thought.

September 2060 – Present Day
Jake Deen – The Red Rocks
Livingsworth, Nevada

"What the fuck, Jake?" Jake heard the sound of Bobby's voice. It seemed muffled—far way.

"Get up!" Jake felt something nudge him lightly in the side. He opened his eyes to find Bobby standing over him. *Shit.*

"Hey! I said get up." This time a soft kick to his leg accompanied the angry words.

"What happened?" Jake asked.

"You tell me!" Bobby exclaimed.

Jake looked around. He was on the floor of Bobby's bar. An empty bottle of whiskey snuggled next to him, and a half empty one stood on the bar among scattered chess pieces. A cracked tumbler lay on its side, coated with brown, syrupy liquid, which was once alcohol.

"Did I drink those?" Jake asked, but he already knew the answer judging by his foul breath. His body shook from dehydration.

"What do you think?" Bobby crossed his arms over his chest, his face reddening.

Jake remembered being pissed off after going to Anna's and running into Sebastián. He remembered going to the bar. Then one shot, two shots, three shots, and then everything went black.

"You're a piece of shit, Jake," Bobby said.

"I'll pay you back." Jake stood up and walked over to the bar to collect the chess pieces.

"It's not about the money," Bobby scolded. "You come into *my* bar, you steal *my* liquor, and then you make a fucking mess. This isn't your place to screw around in. I want you out." Bobby picked up the tumbler and tossed it into a soapy tub behind the bar. Realizing it was cracked, he retrieved it and threw it in the garbage.

"Bobby, I'll clean up. I'll—"

"This isn't up for debate." Bobby placed the half-finished whiskey bottle back on the shelf, lining it up with tens of others.

"I'm sorry, I really fucked up. I promise this will never happen again."

"A promise from a drunk is as empty as his bottle." Bobby's dark eyes were cold.

"Bobby, I will do anything. I will pay you triple, work for free, I'll do whatever you want. Please give me another chance," Jake pleaded and rubbed the back of his head where a familiar throb began to make itself known.

Bobby sighed. "This happens one more time, and I will make sure that you never work in this town again."

September 2060 – Present Day
Jake Deen – The Red Rocks
Livingsworth, Nevada

Jake lay on Anna's bed two days later, admiring her soft curves. He knew he was lucky that Bobby didn't kick him out and that he was able to keep their original arrangement. This left him enough money to visit Anna. Being with her made him feel wanted. It made him feel like he belonged.

"Anna, these past few days . . . what I'm trying to say is . . . I'm happy we met," Jake said, green eyes clear—

happy. He was thankful that Anna didn't stop seeing him after the incident with Sebastián. In his heart he hoped she would stop seeing Sebastián. Him and all the other clients. He needed to give her a reason to.

"Me too." Anna smiled, her lips a perfect, scarlet bow.

"I want to know more about you."

"What do you want to know?" A gust of wind flurried through the bedroom window, and her skin pricked up with goosebumps.

"Where are you from? What are your parents like?"

"They weren't around much. I was raised by my friends, I suppose." Anna took a bobby pin that was clipped to her bra, and put her hair up in a bun.

"But we're not here to talk about me, mister." She poked his chest playfully with her finger. "Remember, time is money." She winked and kissed him. "I want to know more about *you*. You asked me about my parents, now it's my turn to ask you about yours. Tell me about your mom, your dad."

Jake was startled by the question. "My mom . . . I don't remember." Embarrassment and guilt seeped into his heart. "I know she left when I was thirteen, but I don't know why. I thought I'd see her again. I think we were supposed to, but . . ."

Anna patted him on the shoulder.

"That's how fucked up I am. I don't even remember. About a year after she left, my life became a blur. And then, several years after, my dad sent me away."

"And you don't know why?"

Jake's hand touched the scar on the back of his head. "I don't remember," he said, then grabbed the quarter-filled bottle of whiskey from the nightstand next to the bed and chugged the remains.

~ ~ ~

At sunrise, Jake woke up wrapped in a feathery blanket to the hearty smell of bacon and eggs. He walked over to the kitchen, not bothering to clothe himself, and saw that Anna hadn't bothered with clothes either, and that her hair was still ruffled from the night before. The food was almost ready, and there were two cups of coffee on the kitchen table.

"You look well?" Anna's eyes traveled down to his hips. She flipped the bacon with a fork, her breasts shaking lightly with the movement.

"Oh." Jake looked down and saw that he was aroused. "You know, um, it's the morning."

"Yes, it certainly is. Why don't you put your focus elsewhere and make us some toast? The bacon is almost done."

"I'd be happy to." He picked up the baguette lying next to the stove, and a chunk of butter from the battery-operated fridge.

She turned to him right as he was done. "Now you can help me set the table." She smiled at him and he smiled back. The moment felt effortless. It felt right.

"I'd be more than happy to." Jake started taking out the plates and utensils.

"So"—she filled their plates and sat down at the kitchen table—"you said you'll be leaving for some time. Will you be coming back?"

"I'll definitely be back. I like it here," Jake answered, then forked a few bites into his mouth. "I like you."

"What about your life on the road? Living in the moment and getting stranded in the desert?" Anna took a sip of coffee.

Eggs, bacon, toast, and a gorgeous naked woman next to him—life was pretty damn good. "I think it might be time for a change," he said.

"You like what you have now then?" She bit her lip.

They both stopped eating at that moment, and he threw everything off the table with a swift slide of his arm. He pulled Anna up from her chair, gave her a longing kiss, and lay her down.

September 2060 – Present Day
Bill Vos – The Red Rocks
Livingsworth, Nevada

Bill waited for Jake in Bobby's back office. There were no windows, and the off-white walls were bare except for a mounted long-sword behind the desk. It had a black and green leather handle. He noted the new shine on the wooden desk and ran his hand down the smooth surface. The smell of lacquer drifted in the damp air.

After checking the time and realizing he still had a few minutes, Bill picked up a newspaper and leaned back in the leather office chair. The headlines spoke of rampant shooters, protesters attacking police, and unlikely presidential candidates. The date was May 2016.

"You're on time," Bill said as Jake walked in.

"You seem surprised."

I am, Bill thought, and ran his fingers along the edge of his cowboy hat.

"Where are we headed to?" Jake asked, pulling his hair back into a short ponytail.

"Lucyville, then Gerlach, then back here. One way should take about seven to ten days, traveling west from here."

"Great. And the job?" Jake asked.

"Your job is to ride with me," Bill stated. "We're delivering supplies."

"What kind of supplies? Just in case someone asks."

Bill hesitated, then said, "Spices. Spices that were requested by several store and restaurant owners in Gerlach."

"Sounds good to me. When do we leave?"

"Now."

"Let me grab my horse and I'm all set."

"Okay, let's get going. We don't want to be late."

"People need their spices, huh?" Jake grinned.

Bill's solemn expression remained unchanged.

Knock. Knock.

Bobby came in. "The marshal is coming. You better get your shit and leave."

September 2060 – Present Day
Jake Deen – The Red Rocks
Road to Lucyville, Nevada

Jake felt the warm wind in his hair and the equestrian rhythm beneath. The quiet brought a familiar peace, although the heat hadn't broken with the coming of fall. His thoughts wandered to Anna. Was she with someone else? Some other man talking to her, touching her, breathing in her strawberry scent? He coughed and shook his head, but his thoughts hurricaned on. How many clients did she have? He'd seen at least four, but she must have more? Was the woman's voice he'd heard a client too? His thoughts circled like hawks around camouflaged prey. Was it all an act? Did she even like him? Or did she make everyone feel this way? He watched tiny peaks bounce up and down ahead. Winged predators appeared and disappeared in the sky—screeches escaping their beaks intermittently. Jake ignored the nature—Anna on his mind. Did she like him in bed or was that an act too? How many others did she have to compare? Fuck! He needed a drink.

~ ~ ~

The days rolled one into the next. Each day Bill woke Jake at dawn, they packed their camp and ate sticky slabs of gelatin rolled into rice paper. Jake prepped his horse, Delight, and Bill his horse, Morpheus, and they set off to ride the endless Red Rocks roads. At sunset, they'd choose a place to camp, near a rocky hill if they could find one, set up their tents, tend to their horses, and then start a fire and eat dinner in silence. The bitter cold of the nights offset the blazing heat of the days, coaxing them into an early sleep.

On day five, Jake woke before dawn to find Bill already up. He was doing push-ups, and from what Jake could count, at least one hundred of them. Then he switched to sit-ups and squats. Jake didn't doubt Bill went through that routine every day. He thought about joining, but decided he liked sleep more.

As they rode, Jake's anxiety wore on him. How could this man function with no human interaction? Jake was all for deep thought, but it has been five days and they've hardly said a word to each other.

"Hey Bill," Jake said. "What do you do in your spare time?"

Bill looked over at Jake, a hint of amusement in his eyes. "I ride," he said curtly.

It's like pulling teeth with this guy, Jake thought, and considered other topics of conversation. "I noticed you exercise every morning. Can I join you one of these days? I'm feeling a tad out of shape," Jake lied; he was proud of his lean physique and had no interest in working out.

"How about we save our energy for the road? No need for small talk."

"Fine." Jake pouted and rode ahead of Bill, stirring up dust in Bill's direction.

~ ~ ~

That night, they came across an old railroad station whose two remaining walls creaked with every puff of wind. The only words Bill had spoken since the afternoon, were to tell Jake he was going to heed a call to nature, after they had finished setting up camp several feet away from the tracks. Their tents were wedged between what Jake could only call two mounds of dirt. Ahead of them was the hardpan desert, its cracks spidering off toward the bleak horizon.

Jake rubbed his hands before the budding fire. He was on the most silent trip in the world. He leaned in to blow, and watched the flames rise up. Worse than silence, there was no booze. No booze and no one to talk to. His eyes wandered around the camp and settled on Bill's horse, which held his packages. Jake was picking his own deliverables up in Lucyville.

I'll just take a peek while he's still pissing, Jake thought. He stood up and walked over. First, he looked into a large chestnut pack attached to Morpheus' saddle. He peered inside and took out a small cardboard box, one of five. *Could be spices.* There was a wax seal on the box, and he ran his fingers over it, feeling the elaborate curves. He wouldn't be able to replace the seal. He put the box back into the handmade pack.

He stood for a second, listening to hear if Bill was walking back. After, he examined one medium-sized satchel. He thumbed the brown leather and noticed the combination lock on the latch. From his pocket, he took out a bobby pin he had "borrowed" from Anna, inserted it into the lock, then pulled.

Damn it. The lock wouldn't budge. He twisted it one way and then the other, but it didn't shift. Bill would return soon, he should leave it be. He squeezed the lock in frustration. *Click.* It popped open.

Jake moved the flap up and looked inside to find packs of products that sold out in seconds after government supply drops: batteries, bullets, pills, pregnancy tests, and—

"What are you doing?"

Jake turned around. Bill stood across the fire, his eyebrows sinking.

"I was just looking for—"

"Don't lie to me Jake." Bill walked over—tall, brooding. He took Jake's hand off the satchel and twisted it until Jake felt a sharp pain.

"Ouch!"

Bill let him go, then reviewed the contents of the satchel and locked it up.

"Bill, I didn't mean to, I just . . ." Jake looked down at the ground, it was what he used to do when his parents scolded him, before his mom left and everything went to shit.

"Tell me, what *were* you doing?"

"I wanted to know what was in there." *Booze, for example.*

"In my previous line of work, a man once told me that the less I knew about the job, the better. Do as you're told, earn your money, and stay safe."

What line of work was this? Jake wanted to ask, but knew it wasn't the right time.

"You want to know what's in there?"

Jake nodded so hard that his neck cramped up.

"I know you already saw. It's more of the same. Goods from the supply drops. No, it's not legal. Yes, we are at risk if we run into a marshal we can't pay off." Bill fished out a packet from his travel sack and threw it at Jake. The pouch had a smudged brown print on the front. Jake figured it used to be an image of food. He opened it up to smell; whatever was inside had congealed together. Beef and noodles? Squished hamburger? Stew? All three?

"Eat, put out the fire, and sleep. We ride at dawn tomorrow," Bill said and walked toward his tent with his own pouch. Before he got in, he turned around and said, "Next time think about what you are doing, or this will be your last ride with me."

October 2060 – Present Day
Anna Faroe – The Red Rocks
Livingsworth, Nevada

"You are so elegant." A middle-aged brunette sat on Anna's bed, holding a glass of warm white wine. She was a small woman, but those hundred pounds held stories from a hundred worlds. Her name was Gemma, she was a weekly client, and she had been visiting Anna for the three years. She had moved to the Red Rocks right after the area was created. Everyone who wanted to stay in a world with electricity, moved out of the designated Red Rocks area, which covered most of the Rocky Mountain States. But the government didn't move people into the Red Rocks fast enough; there was no policing, and Gemma had had to fend for herself.

"One time, I lived in a supermarket for three months. This was when the government was turning off all the electricity in the Red Rocks, after they had moved everyone out. The place was like Russia in the 1990's (after the wall fell)—complete chaos. I was afraid to leave because of the criminals, vagrants, and volt addicts that came in every day to look for supplies or set up camp for several days. I lived in the vents. I'd come down and see if I could find any food every chance I got when the place was empty. I remember how much I cried when I found a can of baked beans and realized I didn't have an opener. I didn't eat for six straight days that week, until I found a packet of dried pasta underneath the shelf, half-chewed through by rodents or volters."

Anna, in front of her closet, was trying her best to pay attention while picking out a nightgown for Gemma to wear tonight. *Blue? No. Although, Jake would like this one.* A smile crept into her features as she remembered the last time they were together. Lying on the floor, open, true. He was so eager, so boyish. Focus on Gemma, she told herself, upset that her mind had wandered.

Gemma didn't seem to notice that Anna was preoccupied and continued, "You know my husband got addicted to volt back home in the Metropolitans, he tells me he's off it, so I should come home, but I don't believe him. He started taking volt because he was going crazy from the ads, but then he started using it more and more. It was supposed to subdue the visual and hearing senses, but if you take too much, it supposedly gives you a euphoric feeling. No one knew then that it can also make you go crazy. One time he took too much and then he—"

Anna's walked over to her vanity table, noticing a hummingbird statuette standing on it. She didn't have to guess who it was from. He's very sweet, but there are layers of anger underneath, she mused. She'd have to break those layers. What *was* he underneath? A man? Or, after she'd broken the layers, would she find that he was still a little boy?

Anna felt a kiss on her neck, and her skin tingled.

"I like it," Gemma said, pointing to the blue nightgown hanging over Anna's arm.

Anna turned around. "It will look stunning on you." Why was she thinking about Jake when she had a gorgeous woman in front of her? She took a deep breath and caught a glimpse of herself in the mirror. She was a reflection of independence and strength. So why was she not able to compartmentalize?

October 2060 – Present Day
Bill Vos – The Red Rocks
Road to Livingsworth, Nevada

Bill and Jake arrived in Gerlach. It took them one and a half weeks after a short stop in Lucyville, an artsy town filled with old buildings whose walls were covered with murals depicting the tragedy of 8/6/2040. Bill secured the goods for Jake to carry there. In Gerlach, they dropped off their packages and picked up new ones to take back in the direction of Livingsworth.

Bill led the way, passing strip malls filled with empty clothing and furniture stores. Rusty cars and shopping carts cluttered the parking lots, only making way for piles of old garbage. The scent of rotten food and sewage proved strong in the stagnant hot air. Bill veered a mile off the main pathway, weaving between crispy clusters of shrubs poking through the fractured asphalt, until they made it out onto a chalky narrow road. Bill had picked the route in hopes of avoiding travelers.

The road was empty for the first three days. On day four, they made their way into a valley. A group of dirt bikers came toward them. Bill tensed and did a quick once-over of their surroundings. To the left stood a small rolling hill—their escape route—he decided, as the right only held an empty field devoid of life or cover.

Bill's intuitive fingers brushed the butt of his gun, as the riders neared.

"How you fellas doing?" the rider in front spoke with a Southern drawl, his eyes hidden behind thick, yellow goggles. He was scrawny, with thinning hair down to his chest. Three others parked on either side of him a few feet back: two on the right and one on the left.

"We're fine," Bill said and dismounted his horse. Jake followed.

"You need anything?" The rider was chewing tobacco and spit filled up his cheeks.

"What do you have?" Bill asked, pulling down his bandana.

"We have some homemade moonshine." The man took off his goggles, leaving dust-free rings around his eyes. He got off his bike, untied his backpack and fished out a clear glass bottle.

Bill watched Jake's eyes light up. He looked like he was going to snatch it out of the biker's hand.

"We'd rather have water," Bill said.

"Sorry. Moonshine's all we've got." The rider gave him a toothless grin.

Bill looked at Jake. "Fine. We'll take one."

"That would be six." The rider moved closer; he smelled of spoiled fish and urine.

Bill looked carefully at the bottle, then took out two Red Rock notes. A red tint veiled the cotton linen blend of the two note denomination. Bill handed it to the rider. "I'll give you four. The bottle is only three-quarters full."

"Six is better pricing than you can get en 'em towns, full bottle or not." The rider spat.

Bill didn't move. The rider looked annoyed. Sighing, he took a step toward Bill, but instead of taking the money he grabbed Bill's wallet and threw it back to the giant, red-bearded rider behind him.

"Hey!" Bill heard Jake say and watched him run after the wallet. The goggled rider stepped in front of Jake, but Jake pushed Goggles out of the way and went for Red-beard.

Goggles ran up to Bill and raised the bottle over his head. Bill caught his arm and punched him in the gut. He doubled over, breaking the bottle. Bill looked over at Jake and saw that Red-beard—still sitting on his bike—had him in a choke hold. The two riders behind them were moving in to help.

Snap. Slice. Bill felt a sting across his leg. He looked down, finding Goggles waving a knife. Bill kicked the knife-bearing hand. Goggles let out a growl and clawed into Bill's leg with sharp nails. Bill clenched his teeth and shook his leg trying to free himself from the infectious grip.

"Fuck!" Jake's voice rang out after the sound of fist on face.

Bill took out his gun and shot it in the air. "Enough!"

Everyone stopped and stared at Bill.

"You." He pointed at Red-beard. "Give him back my wallet." Red-beard complied. "You." Bill pointed the gun at Goggles. "Get us out another bottle. A full one." Toothless Goggles went for his pack and took out a bottle. "And two of your water canteens."

"I said I have no—"

The Red Rocks

Bill fired a shot next to Goggles' foot, and the little man crawled on all fours to grab the canteens. He placed them next to Bill's horse.

"Now get out of my sight!" Bill yelled.

The riders scrambled onto their bikes and rode off engines roaring, leaving clouds of dirt behind.

Bill turned to Jake after the bikers were little dots on the horizon. "I appreciate you jumping in back there. You have good reflexes."

"That's what a riding partner is for," Jake said.

Bill nodded.

Jake tapped his foot around in the dirt and leaned over to pick something up from the ground. "Look, one of the riders dropped this." He flipped over the shiny object and whispered, *"With you, I'm hole.* It's misspelled. Ha!"

Bill stared at Jake, feeling a mix of gratitude and sadness. Goggles must have swiped the ring from his pocket during the brawl. He would not have forgiven himself if he'd lost it. He gave a small nod and held out his hand.

October 2060 – Present Day
Jake Deen – The Red Rocks
Road to Livingsworth, Nevada

Jake and Bill stopped several hours later and set up camp at an abandoned military post. Red, white, and blue rocks were embedded into the stone walls. Around them, straw covered the ground—a sea of prickly gold. The mountains, sheer and tall, painted a background of neighboring peaks. The sky, taking in the last light from the sun, glittered a blood-orange. They took in the nature around them as sat by the fire eating dinner, then Bill opened the moonshine.

Jake beamed with excitement. Then he remembered. "You told me not to drink on the road." He didn't want to cross any more lines after getting caught going through the satchels.

"If you think you can handle it, we can have a small taste." Bill poured out some of the moonshine on the ground.

"What are you doing?!" Jake exclaimed, bits of saliva shooting out of his mouth. He looked at Bill, his dark hair not neatly combed as usual—remnants of the fight.

"Just in case you get tempted to drink more than you should."

Jake huffed and turned away. Moments later, as the wind picked up, Bill presented the bottle to him, and they drank to keep their bodies warm.

"That's some good stuff!" Jake said after taking a swig, and patted himself on his chest, relieving the burn. It tasted sweet and smelled like apples.

Bill nodded and took a slow sip, then scooped a forkful of spaghetti and meatballs from that night's military pouch dinner. He looked worn, eyes bloodshot, clothes wrinkled.

"So, where were you from in the Metropolitans?" Jake asked.

Bill hesitated, then said, "California."

A moment passed, no one said anything. Jake played around with a twig, drawing stick figures in the dirt. "Which part?"

"Sonoma."

Jake let the thought wash over him and nudged the moonshine bottle over to Bill. "Ah, so you grew up in wine country. I've never been there, but I always—"

"Don't move," Bill said.

"What?" Jake stopped mid-body of stick figure number five. He squinted his eyes. "What's going o—"

Stab! Bill brought a snake up on his knife. It hung upside down, leaking blood. Bill put it on a rock, sliced off the head, and then slithered the skin off in one swift motion.

Jake gulped as the severed head writhed, and Bill kicked it away with his boot. Then he coiled the body around a branch and held it over the fire. They sat in silence again for several minutes.

"So," Jake started the conversation up again. "What year did Sonoma get immersed—get *ad*ttacked?" Jake smiled at his own pun.

"In 2036. I was lucky to have spent my childhood without many ads. It was bad by the end. Virtual ads would pop up from the grapevines, promoting their own wines. Each vine stake was covered in video ads. When you walked by, the ad would talk to you, tell you what type of dinner that wine goes with." Bill paused and rubbed his chin. "It was very odd, come to think of it."

More than a one word answer, the moonshine must be working, Jake thought. He watched Bill turn the snake slowly for an even cook.

"You had your own winery?" Jake asked, and got up to grab his blanket as the fire shifted with the howling wind.

"My parents did."

"Are they still around?" Jake settled back into his nook and rolled a cigarette from his tobacco pouch.

"No." Bill brought the smoking snake out of the fire. "No one is there anymore; that's why I am here," he said in a somber tone. He cut the snake into pieces and handed over a plateful. Jake took the seared reptile, hesitated, then bit into it.

Fucking delicious! Jake chowed down the meat in seconds and took a sip of moonshine. He saw that Bill had also finished his portion and was rolling his thumb over the ring he had recovered from the ground earlier, it caught the last rays of sunlight.

"What was her name?" Jake asked, admiring the white gold setting which enveloped a princess cut diamond. His father had taught him as much. He had owned a pawn shop back in the Metropolitans.

"Emily," Bill said, holding the ring in front of him. "But no one ever called her that. She was always Emmy."

"Where did you two meet?" Jake nudged the bottle over to Bill who seemed to talk more after a swig.

"At the university. I can't believe I almost blew her off when we first met."

"Really?"

"It was my second year in college. My parents always wanted me to go school and get a degree. Unfortunately, they didn't get the chance to see me graduate." Bill paused and Jake stayed quiet, watching invisible bugs make shadows around the fire. "I stayed at the winery, and it wasn't until the vines started dying off that I decided to sell it and leave for college," he continued after a moment. "I failed three of my classes freshman year, but was determined to make up for it the year after, so I went to the library every single day.

After two months, the days all blurred together—all days except for that day. I remember everything from that day like it was yesterday. The walk, the hot weather, I even remember the ads I saw. One was for a new cereal bar, another for a sports car—that's the type of person I was profiled as, I guess."

"Sports car? Were you still allowed to drive?" Jake's eyes went wide like the eyes of a child opening a present.

"No, I think all cars had to be self-driving since 2025. Anyway, I sat down at the first ad-free table and got to work. About a half-hour later, a girl came up to me and asked what I was reading. I told her it was *History of Technology: 2000 – 2010*."

"2000, so long ago," Jake said.

Bill nodded and continued, "She told me to read the Metropedia, the free world wide encyclopedia. I told her I didn't like shortcuts, and that if she wasn't serious about her education, then that was fine, but *I* wanted to do the work fully, properly. Then I told her to leave me alone."

"Ouch."

"She walked away, and I realized I was in the wrong. I ran after her, and when she turned around, I knew she was the girl I was going to marry." Bill opened his hand and took the ring in his thumb and forefinger, turning it around from one side to the other. His expression was a mix of love and pain.

"It's a beautiful ring," Jake offered.

"It was my mother's," Bill said, and his lips began to curve on one side into a half-smile. "It was from her previous engagement. She never told Dad that she had kept it." Bill held the ring up to the light and touched the inside. "I decided to inscribe the ring because I wanted it to be one of a kind. The phrase was supposed to be *with you, I'm whole*, but they screwed up and put *hole—h-o-l-e*—instead! We always laughed about it. I never ended up getting it changed." Bill chuckled at the memory.

October 2060 – Present Day
Jake Deen – The Red Rocks
Livingsworth, Nevada

Seven days later, when they reached Livingsworth, Bill left two small packages with Jake, asking him to deliver them to Tonopah and Goldfield, two nearby towns about four day's ride south of Livingsworth. Bill told him to try not to talk to anyone on the road and to avoid the highway.

Jake planned to stop by Anna's before riding out, but first went to Bobby's to freshen up. He was surprised at how much he had missed the place.

"Welcome back," Bobby shouted. He stood next to a short girl with blond curly hair. She kissed him on the lips and disappeared into the kitchen behind the bar. Bobby smiled and walked over to Jake who gave him a thumbs up. The place was empty but for two regulars sitting up at the bar, playing chess and drinking whiskey.

"So, how was the trip?" Bobby asked, a familiar twinkle in his eye.

"It was great, but exhausting. It's good to be back."

"I bet, over two weeks on the road can take it out of you. On the other hand, it's the perfect amount of time for you to start missing us." Bobby winked. "Here, have a shot and beer on the house." He brought out an aged bourbon from a cabinet beneath the register.

Jake started to nod, but then surprised himself. "You know. I think I'll pass this time." Maybe he could cut down on the drinking while he was *off* the road too. He hadn't had a sip since the biker moonshine, and he felt good.

Bobby raised an eyebrow in surprise. "Really? Well, suit yourself." He poured himself two fingers.

"Well, actually—" Jake began as the door opened and a man walked in: tall, stocky, with overgrown hair and a badge. Bobby muttered something under his breath.

"Bobby Kennedy. Well, well, well." The man sat down on a stool and put his badge on the bar. Jake moved farther down. "I see you have some new liquor inventory." The man was pointing at the row of bottles on the shelves. Bobby's face tensed. "May I see the receipt for those?" Bobby walked into the back.

"What's your name, young man?" The stocky man turned his attention to Jake.

"Jake."

"Well, Jake. I hope you know that if you don't have receipts for government-issued goods, bad things can happen to you." He slapped his hand down on the bar and glasses rattled.

Bobby walked back in with several pieces of paper. He ran his fingers down his goatee while the marshal looked at them.

"Bobby, Bobby, Bobby," he said and threw the papers back. "Do you think I was born yesterday? The dates are off here."

"Are they?" Bobby asked. "I didn't notice." He clenched the receipts.

"I'm sure you can find *some* other papers back there." Bobby left and came back with a stack of Red Rock notes.

"That's more like it!" The marshal belched and stood up. "Until next time." He bowed and walked out.

"Fucker," Bobby said. "He's new in town." He crumpled the receipts and threw them in the trash.

"What would he do if you didn't pay?" Jake asked.

"Put me in the temp jail? Report me? Shoot me? Who knows? I don't fuck around with the shitty law here. Marshals are elected by the fucking government officials in the Metropolitans who don't care about anything here in the Red Rocks. There are no ads here, which means no money. They turn to corruption to line their pockets. That's the price we pay for wanting to live in an ad-less world."

"Well, here." Jake took out a wad of cash from his travel bag and handed it to Bobby. It was everything he owed Bobby, to the note.

Bobby counted and nodded.

"I'll be doing more deliveries for Bill, so there will be more where that came from. I'll pay you rent and I'll buy your horse, Delight. Anyway I can help, I will."

"Thanks," Bobby said, but he looked distracted. "Hey Jake?" He said after a moment.

"Yeah?"

"Next time you ride out, can you do me a favor?"

"Sure."

"Get me a battery cassette recorder."

October 2060 – Present Day
Anna Faroe – The Red Rocks
Livingsworth, Nevada

"Jake, I understand where you're coming from, but I can't." Anna and Jake were sitting on her bed, she in her robe and he in his briefs. Five candles lit the room and baked the air with the scent of apples and cloves—the scent of fall.

"Anna, but I have money now, and I'm about to get more on my trips to Tonopah and Goldfield. Can't you cancel your appointments? I will pay for all of their time *and* my time. I want to spend the next three days with you." Jake inched closer to Anna.

She stood up and walked to her dresser. Sitting down in front of the mirror, she began to brush her hair. She was already too close, with him filling her thoughts. *He's trying to cage me.* "Jake, it's not about the money. I can't cancel my clients for you," she stated firmly.

He walked over to her, dropped down to his knees and clasped his hands together in prayer. "Anna, when I was away, all I could think about is you. I missed you so much. I want to see more of you." He turned her chair to face him and hugged her legs, putting his head on her lap.

He's so stubborn. "Jake, I am true to my craft, and true to helping people. Many of my clients have been through a crisis, and our sessions help them work through it."

"It's just a few days."

"Schedules are important."

"Anna . . ." He stood up and kissed her head, then neck, and she felt her whole body tense. A part of her wanted him to leave. He was asking for too much. But the other part, the part that wanted his touch, the part that wanted to make him whole, let him stay. He took off her silk robe and led her to the bed.

She did not cancel her clients, but on their last night together, Anna did not make him pay.

October 2060 – Present Day
Jake Deen – The Red Rocks
Tonopah and Goldfield, Nevada

Jake left three days later, and the ride was tough, the wind—bone-chilling. Jake passed a deserted gas station and a superstore. Its rectangle sign teetered back and forth on a single wire. A "W" and an "M" were still visible through the cracked vinyl. He found a broken pack of cigarettes in front, surprised no one had collected it. When he picked it up, a Red Rock widow crawled out of it. He dropped the pack and ran into the store.

The store was huge; it used to have everything from home and garden supplies to food. The shelves looked sad with nothing on them. The floor was sticky and coated with broken glass. Jake felt a tinge of nostalgia for the days when he could buy everything in one place.

As Jake wandered from one aisle to the next, his mind focused on Anna. Her strawberry smell. Her eyes. Her mouth. Her soft velvet touch. Her touch . . . her touching others. If I can get enough money, I know I can convince her to quit, he thought. But somewhere deep inside, he felt doubt.

Doubt once again that a person he loved, like his mother and father, didn't really love him back.

Not finding anything in the superstore except a dirty American flag print towel and an empty pack of condoms, he kept on moving.

On his second day, Jake came across a large hexagonal dome made from a web of aluminum bars; it was covered by a plastic tarp. Inside were two mattresses, pillows, blankets, and a cooler. In the corner, he found a small wooden chest filled with packets of rice and marinated canned beef. He moved them and discovered a pack of Red Rocks pellets. The wrapper had two mountain peaks and their slogan: *RR: The Best Kind of Rock*. On the back, a yellow star promoted: *Extra Gluten*.

Too much dust and too many spider webs for someone to be living here, Jake thought. He should set up camp in this place and get away from the weather. He took the Red Rocks pellets and the rice, and placed them in his travel sack; the cans were too heavy. He tied up Delight outside, and set up his tent.

~ ~ ~

Jake reached Tonopah four days after leaving Livingsworth. It was small and dirty, trash and human waste littered the streets and gutters. He passed a row of crumbling outlet stores; the smell of urine filled the air. At a hotel with a giant clown on the front, he gave the packages to a man with a long beard and thinning hair. Their minimal exchange made Jake feel unwelcome, but then again, so did the rest of the town.

He made good time on the road to Goldfield. It was a breath of fresh air compared to Tonopah.

Goldfield was clean. It radiated with tall, bright buildings, and overflowed with people. As he walked down the street, many of the artsy stores and venues piqued his interest. Two Native American men dressed in leather vests and jeans stood in front of a smoke shop and called out to him, "Come here, son, and we'll show you the true art of smoking. This tobacco will open your spiritual self."

Jake shook his head.

Next, he passed brothel where a blonde, a redhead, and a brunette came out in matching black lace tops and shorts. The redhead looked at Jake's horse and started petting it.

"What a pretty horse, and what a handsome man." She flirted. "Come play with us, won't you?"

"No thanks, ladies."

"Don't you like what you see?" One girl scooted down her top, flashing her ample cleavage.

"Yes, but I have a—" Jake frowned. *What should I call her?* "Someone," he said.

"She or he can't be that important if you're not wearing a ring," the blonde chimed in.

"She is," Jake said, and pulled Delight behind him. As the girls tugged at him, he realized that the second delivery was in their venue. Pregnancy tests and medication, he bet. He delivered the goods quickly, picked up the cash, and walked out.

Following the street, Jake's mouth watered when he saw a whiskey merchant in a wooden booth passing out samples. No, he told himself and kept walking. He hadn't taken a sip since he got on the road, and he meant to keep the streak going. Gotta get some rest, he thought, and then back home, home to Anna. Home . . .

Jake walked to the nearest hotel. Inside, the walls were bare except for a deer head above the check-in counter. It stared him down with empty eyes. He shivered and thought about leaving, but decided to give the place a shot. He made his way to the bar, away from the intruding gaze of the mounted taxidermy.

"Can I get a menu?" Jake asked.

"You betcha! The food here is pretty good and comes out fast, if I say so myself." A pimply barkeeper handed him a grease-smeared menu. The food was more expensive than he would have preferred, but Jake peeked at the other plates and saw that it was worth it. They must own their own farm and cattle, he thought. This wasn't that shit concentrate meat from the government stores.

"You know what? I think I'll just have whatever he's having." Jake pointed to the young man sitting next to him, eating steak and grilled green tomatoes; the smell made Jake's stomach growl.

"And to drink?"

"What do you have that's non-alcoholic?"

She looked at him as if no one had ever asked her this question before. "We did just get something called club soda delivered, but I've never had it."

"I'll take it."

The Red Rocks

The food came out fast and Jake dug in. After his meal, he picked his teeth with a toothpick. He turned his attention back to the remains of his plate and club soda.

"You have any newspapers lying around?" he asked the bartender, and she handed him what she had.

She commented, "It's only a year old."

"Can't believe they still make these," he said.

"Why?"

"They only make them for the Red Rocks. They never get delivered on time. Not really even sure who provides the content."

"They don't have them in the Metropolitans?"

"No, they haven't had newspapers in print since before I was born."

"I've never been to the Metropolitans, so I wouldn't know." The waitress shrugged and hurried off to serve another table.

Never been to the Metropolitans? What a crazy thought that is. To live in the Red Rocks without ever knowing the modern comforts of life, the technologies, the ads . . . Perhaps that's a good thing, Jake thought. He flipped through the first couple of pages, chewing the last of his now soggy tomatoes. As he was finishing up an article about a new ad you could put onto your teeth by applying a clear coating, he heard the door slam and looked up. An old man stumbled towards the bar and sat down facing away from Jake. He ordered two shots of green liquor.

Absinthe? Jake thought. Hope he knows he's not getting the woodworm with it. Although, you never really know in the Red Rocks. Sometimes you get that little surprise and it's either really good, or really great! He smiled to himself and watched the old man for a while. The man took one shot after another. Looks like someone's got a habit, Jake thought. Then he remembered when Bill had picked him up: his body shaking, insides burning, and the kind of chills that could kill you. He was no one to judge.

Jake paid, rolled a cigarette, and left the bar. He stood outside smoking and watched the sun inch down toward its hiding place behind a rocky fortress. It glittered off the red brick buildings and copper signs. It was warm, and yet, Jake felt a mild discomfort.

"Mind if I grab a light from you?" a scratchy voice behind him asked.

"Sure," Jake said, but when he saw the man's face, he dropped his book of matches. It was the old man from the bar, and his reaction mirrored Jake's—eyes widening in recognition.

"How are you doin' tonight?" the old man asked.

Jake's heart raced, a thin layer of sweat forming on his forehead, then his palms and underarms. His mind went blank from shock, and he didn't realize he was speaking. "I'm doing quite well, and yourself?"

"As good as can get, Son." The old man smiled.

September 2045 ~ 15 Years Ago
Jake Deen – Metropolitans
San Francisco, California

Five days after his eighteenth birthday, Jake stood looking at the commercial-covered platforms near the train tracks. Logos, trademarks, taglines. It was like an endless jigsaw puzzle, each ad piece fit perfectly next to the others. No white space, no space to clear one's mind.

A pop-up jumped up next to him; it was a hologram of a young girl selling an organic soft drink. She was Jake's height and age. She had olive skin, full breasts, dark hair, and blue eyes—a combination of every woman he had looked up on his computer when his adolescent body craved sex. Except she was prettier, more perfect, created for no one else but him to see.

She purred at him with promises of satisfaction. Despite the softness of her voice, his head was pounding from a bruise sustained days earlier. He didn't recall what happened. He pressed a button on his shirt and the pop-up girl disappeared, the pixels vanishing.

Jake's father, David, walked over and handed him a snack printed from a vending machine. He was medium height, his belly rolled over his belted jeans, and light-brown hair fell over his eyes, which carried heavy circles underneath. His clothes displayed multicolored images that changed each time a new person walked by—apparel ad space, a recent addition to the advertising market in the Metropolitans.

"I don't want to go to the Red Rocks." Jake fought back tears of anger, and the thumping in his head amplified. "Please don't make me leave."

The Red Rocks

David sighed and Jake felt his dad's hot, whiskey-stained breath on his face.

"You're going and that's final." David's face muscles tensed.

"Why are you doing this to me?" Jake squeezed his head lightly with his hands in hopes of easing the hammering.

"You need to leave. It's for your own good." David coughed.

"Do I? Did you finally belt me to the point of amnesia and now you're trying to save your own ass?" Jake stomped and an elderly woman passing by sped up her pace.

"Keep your voice, down," David said, his face an ode to misery.

"Or what?" Jake crossed his arms over his chest.

David didn't explain. He grabbed Jake by the arm and led him to the loading zone.

"Dad, please. I don't want to go. Let me stay, I'll do anything." Jake tried a different approach.

"No. You have to go, and no matter what you do. You cannot come back. You hear me?" David shook Jake by the shoulders.

Jake opened his mouth to speak, but no words came out.

"It's time," David said, motioning to the train door as the conductor spoke in the background.

Jake climbed onto the neon-blinking high-speed train, walked over to the first bar cabin, and, when the server wasn't looking, stole a bottle of cheap rum.

October 2060 – Present Day
Jake Deen – The Red Rocks
Goldfield, Nevada

Jake's head screamed with confusion; he clutched his fists. *This can't be happening.* His throat went dry and he was unable to utter a single word. He sucked at his cigarette, despite the harshness, like it was his last.

"Jake, it's been so long." His father lit his own cigarette after picking up the matches from the ground.

"You are mistaken, sir." Jake turned, flicked away his butt.

"Jake, my son, please don't walk away." His father moved toward him, but Jake stepped away.

"Why not?" Jake responded bitterly. "You did!"

Pain painted Jake's father's weathered face. He stood an inch shorter than Jake, his once-fit body altered by years of abuse. "This is very sudden, but after all these years, I just can't believe . . . I can't believe it's you." Tears welled up in his father's green eyes—Jake's green eyes. A couple walking into the restaurant looked over at them, pricking their ears. Jake and his father moved out of their way and walked onto the deck of the hotel to the right of the entrance.

"I've searched for you everywhere, and to find"—Jake's father let out a sob and held out a trembling hand—"I'm so happy to see you."

Jake was overwhelmed by a feeling he couldn't pin down. A child's instinct to hug his father tugged somewhere deep inside, but it was squashed by anger. "I don't want to do this, David," Jake said through gritted teeth.

"Jake, I missed you so much. Please give me a chance to explain."

"Explain what exactly? Explain how you sent me away? How you went 'looking' but never found me in all these years?" he yelled, nostrils flaring.

A group of people watching a juggler in the street turned to look in their direction, but quickly turned back after Jake waved his fist at them.

"There are many things in life that I have done that I'm not proud of, Son, but leaving you, is by far my number one regret."

"I don't believe you." Jake spat.

A tear dropped from David's left eye. "I tried to find you, I swear. I looked and looked, but I could not find you in Livingsworth, the city where you were supposed to go."

Jake's eyes were full of fury. "I never made there! Not until now! And how did you expect me to find anything when I had never even left the state at that time?"

"I'm sorry, Son."

"Sorry doesn't change shit!" Jake kicked the deck's wiry fence, causing the table and chairs to wobble.

"Please Jake, let's talk about this."

"What, you want to talk about you sending me off? Or you want to catch up and see how my last fifteen years were?" Jake shook his head in disgust. "You know it amazes me that even after being away from your poison, even after all of this time, I still somehow managed to end up exactly like you—a piece of shit drunk. At least I was smart enough not to have kids; my life is the only life I'm fucking up."

David's eyes reddened once more and he looked away. "I never meant for everything to fall apart."

"But you did. With your gambling and your drinking and your whores after Mom left! That's exactly what you meant to do!"

"There are things you don't know, Son. Please give me a chance to explain. I promise to leave you alone, if you just give me this one chance." The old man cleared his throat and spat thick, snail-like mucus on the ground. His eyes were tired and watery. He looked so thin and frail, Jake almost felt sorry for him. Almost.

"Bye, David." Jake jumped the metal railing and made his way to the side of the hotel where the stables were. He heard David start to cough.

"I'll tell you what happened to Mom," David shouted.

Fuck, Jake thought. I can't fucking trust him, but . . . he's my father. This was his only chance to reconnect, to learn what happened to his mom, to get answers. He looked at David. "Fine. I'll give you thirty minutes. But I need a drink."

He's in my life for less than ten minutes, he thought, and I'm off the wagon.

The dim eyes looked back at Jake and something came alive in them. "I think a drink is a wonderful idea." He pulled out a full bottle of whiskey from underneath his black velvet coat. Jake remembered that coat, his mother had given it to his father a long time ago—a time when they were happy.

Jake and David situated themselves on the deck, at a small table. A porcelain plate sat in the middle with a candle stuck to it—a prisoner to its own wax. David produced two portable 4oz tin cups from the other side of his coat, blew into them, and wiped them down with a checkered handkerchief. He filled both cups to the brim. Jake swallowed the contents in one gulp. The welcoming sting trickled through his insides. David poured them a second round, but Jake pushed his away.

"Son, I never meant . . . I wasn't . . ." David trailed off.

Jake felt the heat rise in his body. "Start talking. I am here, giving you a chance to explain, so why don't you make an effort and stop your delaying bullshit!"

"I deserve that." David picked up his cup, a tremor in his hand. "You know, your mom . . . she was . . . sick."

Jake eyes widened, but deep inside he knew. "I sort of knew, I guess." Fuzzy moments from his childhood clawed their way into his mind.

"I didn't know how to handle it. She was fine one minute and sick the next." David coughed, looking away.

Jake saw the pain in his father's eyes, but pressed on anyway. "What was it? You never told me."

"Admania, same as the rest of the world. The visual and mental impact of the ads, the noise, the invasion of privacy was too much for so many, she was no different." David exhaled and took a drink, his eyes clouding over.

Thousands of questions rose up in Jake's head, yet he said nothing.

"We tried medication, therapy, group therapy, but nothing worked. In the end, we decided it would be better if she moved in with her mom in the country, a less ad-saturated place."

"Sounds to me like you both just gave up," Jake said, and watched a dog run by, frantically trying to catch up to its owners who were paying no mind.

"Believe me, Jake, I tried for a long time to get your mother better. Her life was surreal. She said it felt like her life was someone else's and everyone else's at the same time. She couldn't see or hear just one ad at a time. She saw all of them at the same time on different wavelengths. She compared it to being in parallel universes at the same time, following all the different paths at the same time, and seeing where all the paths led to—all at the same time.

One time I found her in the middle of the street, staring at the top-to-bottom ad-covered wall. The ad space booked for years to come. She stood there, taking one step forward, then one step back. Cars swerved around her, but she kept moving one step forward, then one step back. I yelled at her to go to the sidewalk, but she couldn't hear me. Later, when I asked her what she was doing, she told me she was trying to get stuck in one of the commercials that she saw on the ad-covered wall because at least during the duration of that commercial, she would be able to focus, she wouldn't have to live through all of the other commercials. The world she lived in now, her mind was constantly restarting, refocusing, reliving. She was searching for peace."

Jake looked at the ground. "I didn't know that's why she moved away. I thought it was because of me somehow, like

I was bad child. Why did we never visit her? Where is Mom now? Do you still talk to her?"

David exhaled and started to roll a cigarette. Finally, he said, "I'm sorry, Son, but she passed away. I thought you knew."

"What?!" Jake cried out. He had suspected as much, but the finality of those words felt like a million of pieces of glass boring into his skin. "How?" Jake's voice cracked, his eyes weakened.

"8/6/2040, she was part of it. I'm sorry, Son. She just couldn't handle it. The sickness finally got the best of her." David's face expressed torment.

Jake sat there, silent.

"I blame myself. I didn't see the signs of the sickness until it was too late."

"How did she do it?"

"Jake, I don't think—"

"How?!"

"She jumped. From a cliff. Five others." David polished off another cup.

Jake stayed quiet. He was shivering, but it wasn't because of the weather.

"At least she wasn't alone, she did it on 8/6/2040 with all the other millions of people around the world. There was a group called ad-fighters. They connected through a written publication. We think she got recruited on the streets when she was in one of her admania spells wandering around. Someone must've seen her and signed her up. Everyone who signed up would receive a newsletter every two weeks. At first, the purpose was to discuss ways to manage admania, but then, as the disease got worse for so many, the topic switched to freeing yourself from admania. That's when they picked a date, and then . . ." David put his face in his hands.

"This is bullshit. Life is such bullshit."

"I saw it on the news."

"Everyone saw it, David. People throwing down their electronics, holding hands, jumping from cliffs around the world, drinking poison, shooting themselves! The fucking terror of it all." Jake grabbed the bottle and took three large swallows.

David looked up. "I'd like to think there was some purpose. It helps me cope."

"What purpose could there possibly be?" Jake's face transformed from sadness to exasperation. A bird flew by, leaving behind a tiny white puddle on their table.

"I'd like to think she did it for us. A message to the world that it was no longer functioning. That we needed to create places like the Red Rocks, free from electricity, free from the ads, to keep the world going."

Jake could see that David's face had changed. Even through the dim light, it was red, it was anger.

"If those damn politicians would have just given us a fucking break! Those dirty assholes. Studies were done; they knew that if they turned the ads down just a bit, had an ad-free day, it could've saved so many people from the sickness. But they couldn't do it. Politicians are businessmen now, only caring about their own personal gain. They could've just given up a little bit of profit to make some of the ads go away. No, this wasn't good enough for them. They needed their goddam toilet made of gold and their shit made into gold statues. The lives of millions paid for them to live like royalty. They're worse than the jerks who . . ."

As David rambled on, Jake felt the world shrink into darkness, his heart crumbled. He couldn't breathe. He couldn't think. When the whiskey was almost finished, he said, "I don't know what you want from me."

David downed his drink. "I was a shitty father after your mother left, I was broken. I spent nights in bed crying, wishing *I* was the one afflicted, that *I* was the one sick. I knew she was a better mother than I was a father, and there was nothing I could do."

"Nothing you could do? Put down the damn bottle and take care of your son!" Jake's yelling startled a cat near the hotel and it sprinted away with a hiss.

"I tried to be a good father, but it was hard to raise you alone. I realized, then, how much I had taken your mother for granted. You changed too, after she left, you were . . . you were . . . a handful." A shadow crossed over David's face.

Jake shook his head and tapped his foot.

"It was my fault for not being there. I'd drink, and when I was drunk, I couldn't be a parent. I wasn't strong enough to keep you in line."

"I'm not a fucking animal. I was a kid, confused, rebellious, whatever. You should've been a father. You shouldn't have sent me away."

David looked off to the side, an unsaid truth lurking beneath his expression. "I tried so hard and you kept"—David coughed—"you kept getting into trouble. I had to send you away, to the Red Rocks, to Livingsworth, it was the best I could do at the time." David fidgeted and put one dirty pant leg over the other.

"Don't lie to me. As soon as she left, you didn't want to be a father. You just wanted me out so you could binge, gamble, and booze up with your whores! Meanwhile beating the fuck out of me!" Jake pounded his hand on the table.

"I'm not asking for forgiveness, I just wanted you to know."

"Well, now I do. You weren't there for Mom, and you weren't there for me. So I guess not much has changed." Jake knew what he said was hurtful, but it was fair.

"I love you very much and I loved your mother very much." David took the bottle and poured the rest of the whiskey to himself. "It has to be a sign that we ran into each other after all of these years. I'd like to see you again, I want to be a part of your life . . . if you let me."

"How can I?" Jake snorted. "Would you?"

"I know you're angry and upset. I understand if you're not ready right now. Please, just think about it."

"You're right. I'm not ready." He pushed his cup across the table.

"I just thought, I just—"

"What David? What did you think? That you can just come into my life and make everything go back to normal? That we'd be son and father again?"

"Take all the time you need. Here's where I'm staying." David got out a wrinkled piece of paper and pen from his pocket and scribbled down his address. "I hope we can see each other again."

"Don't count on it," Jake said, and walked away, leaving the piece of paper with David.

October 2060 – Present Day
Bill Vos – The Red Rocks
Kingman, Nevada

Bill rode to Kingman to meet Tommy, the rich, fat, bald man he hated, but without whom he would not be able to send money to the Metropolitans. Their meetings tended to be brief and simple, but something felt different this time around. He had a bad feeling.

He arrived at Kingman minutes before the meeting. This time they met at Tommy's office where the walls were covered in black and white pictures of the banker shaking hands with long gone celebrities. The brisk room smelled of cigar smoke and pungent cologne.

"Listen Bill, I have some news for you," Tommy said after they had discussed the details of the deliveries. "I received a message that your relative, or whoever you're sending money to, is getting worse. They treated her for all they could at the hospital, but apparently it's not enough. She needs surgery."

The prick didn't have the decency to tell me as soon as I came in, Bill thought. Always business first. "Can you find out how much the surgery will cost?"

"I don't know, it's going to be a pretty penny, though. Not enough deliveries you can do to get that kind of money." As Tommy spoke, shiny drops of spittle flew to polish the wooden table. "I'll tell you what though." He cleared his throat. "I'll do you a solid. I'll pay for it and you'll owe me one. Easy as that." Tommy grinned.

Bill clenched his jaw. Every part of his being told him to decline, but it was Emmy's last relative. Her mother. He had promised Emmy he would take care of her. This was the only way he could send her money. If he contacted her in the Metropolitans directly, he could subject her to a raid or even worse, imprisonment. After he left the Metropolitans, he knew he had to cut ties with family, friends—everyone in his life—for their own safety. The military didn't take abandonment lightly, they would keep wiretaps on all of them, even ten years later.

"Okay," Bill said, and they shook hands.

"You can't say I don't care of my own."

But it's always for a price, Bill thought.

October 2060 – Present Day
Anna Faroe – The Red Rocks
Livingsworth, Nevada

Anna was taking a stroll by the Livingsworth Base, a large field behind the Town Square, fenced in with barbed wire. The drones dropped off supplies there monthly, and she liked to watch the little specs in the sky send down parachutes with impact resistant boxes. It was a clear day and birds were chirping. A man and a little girl stood next to her, watching. She heard the girl ask, "Daddy, why aren't airplanes dropping off our food?"

"Because, honey, airplanes can project ads, and the people in charge don't want that here." He bounced her up and down on his hip.

The exchange made Anna smile. The man's warm eyes reminded her of Jake's. He'll be back soon, she thought, and then . . . She breathed in deeply and crossed her arms.

Bystanders were taking their places for the show, and the deputies came out, signaling the start. Several minutes later, a robotic buzz came from above, and little black packages floated down one by one.

She thought about Jake. Was she making a mistake by keeping him as a client? She knew she was getting too close, but she couldn't seem to help herself, she missed his calloused hands and wild hair.

November 2060 – Present Day
Anna Faroe – The Red Rocks
Livingsworth, Nevada

Three days later, Anna walked out of her house to find Jake fumbling with the reins, attempting to tie them to her white porch posts, leavings smears of grime. Delight fought against him with nods and neighs.

"Anna!" Jake screamed, "I'm home!" He stumbled up the three steps towards to front door, holding onto the rails.

"Jake! What are you doing? She put his arm over her shoulder and brought him over to her couch.

"Delight . . . he's tied"—hiccup!—"tied up."

"I'll bring him to the back. Stay here," Anna said, her tone reproachful.

After tending to Delight, she came back in, lit a vanilla jasmine candle, and placed it on the coffee table. Then she went into the kitchen and poured them both a glass of iced tea; she was glad that she was able to get batteries for her fridge this time. She took out a detoxifying charcoal tablet and crushed it into his tea, hoping it would sober him up.

She sat down next to Jake and studied him for a moment, his pale face weary, his green eyes sad. His hair was lumped together into one unkempt strand. "Your trip wasn't pleasant, was it?"

"How did you"—Jake stood up, then sat back down—"how did you know?"

"What happened?"

"I don't know how to say this." Jake looked at the floor. "I ran into David . . . my father."

"Your father?" Anna asked in surprise. "I thought you two were estranged."

"We were. It was weird. It was all very sudden." Jake put his head in his hands. "I'm sorry, I didn't even take a bath before coming here, I just . . . I just . . ."

"Don't worry about that." Anna moved closer to him on the couch. She didn't mind his traveled smell. "How did you find each other?"

"He said he hung around this area a long time looking for me. He even said he looked for me in Livingsworth, but I don't believe him." Jake kicked the floor with his foot.

She rubbed his thigh in comfort. "Family can be difficult. There is no shame in being angry with someone who has wronged you."

"I know, but I felt weak, like I'd caved again. I stayed and talked to him." Jake leaned into her, placing his head against her shoulder.

"But you haven't forgiven him. I'm sure he understands that. Do you regret speaking to him?" She kissed his forehead.

Jake shook his head. "No, he um . . . he told me about my mom. She was part of 8/6/2040. She fucking jumped. She left to get better, and then she jumped. She left, and then he left . . ."

"I'm so sorry, Jake," Anna said and picked up his tea cup encouraging him to drink.

"I think deep down I knew, but I needed to hear it."

Anna nodded. "Knowing is better than not knowing."

"At least she wasn't alone," Jake mimicked his father's words.

They sat in silence and Anna ran her hand up and down his back, making him relax.

"Some people say that if The Red Rocks hadn't been created after 8/6/2040, larger catastrophes would strike, and the world would fall apart," she commented, easing off the pressure.

"Yes, David said something similar."

"But it doesn't make it easier, does it?"

"No, it doesn't." He lifted his head and looked into her eyes. "But you do." He leaned in for a kiss. "I want to be with you, Anna. Our time is limited on this earth, and I don't want to lose you or share you. I want us to be together."

Anna looked into Jake's eyes. "You mean a lot to me, Jake. I want to help you, but—"

"But what, Anna? But what? I am not good enough? I'll pay for everything, I'll keep you safe. I'll do anything! *Anything!*"

Anna blinked, and wet mascara stained her cheek. "I cannot do what you are asking me to do, Jake."

"Why can't you? Do you feel like that with everyone? Am I just one of them? How do I know for sure?"

"No, Jake, you are not like everyone else."

"Then why? Why can't we be like normal people in love! You know Bill, my riding partner? He was in love! So much in love that he still carries his wife Emmy's ring with him everywhere he goes! To him, he's whole with her. The ring even says: *with you, I'm hole*! H-O-L-E HOLE!" He laughed, then his face morphed into pleading anger. "That's not the point! With you, Anna, I feel like I'm whole! Why am I not enough for you?" Jake's face was full of hurt.

"Jake I—"

"Anna please! I need you."

"Jake, you can stay with me tonight, and for the rest of the week."

"And your clients?"

"I'll rework my schedule. They won't be here when you are here."

"What about after this week?"

"I will see what I can do."

"Is that supposed to be enough?"

"I don't know, Jake. That's up to you."

Jake looked away, then turned to her and gently pinned her down, holding her hands above her with one arm. She did not resist as he pulled up her slip.

December 2060 – Present Day
Jake Deen – The Red Rocks
Road to Manti, Utah

Bill called on Jake one month later, leaving a note at Bobby's along with cash for his deliveries to Tonopah and Goldfield. Manti, a city east of Livingsworth, was their next destination.

They set out early one morning, Delight and Morpheus loaded with numerous sacks, each tagged, knotted or sealed. The clouds spilled tiny raindrops, slowly darkening the riders' clothes and turning dirt to mud. The bushes, trees, and grass looked sad as they fought to stay erect against the wind and water.

Jake couldn't stop thinking about his father. *He didn't give me a choice, that manipulative asshole! I need to see him if I want any memories of Mom.* Jake was close with his mother, the love she gave him was irreplaceable. His father could help him remember her. He coughed. *I need to focus. I don't need to make the final decision now.*

After two days on the road, both men looked ragged. The rain had stopped, but they had to slow their pace due to the rough wet earth irritating the horses' hooves.

I should meet with him again. At least for my mother. But how can I without him carving his way into my life? I should ask Bill maybe. Maybe . . . maybe not.

Near midday of day five, they passed a narrow road between two hills. Bill stopped suddenly, and Jake came up beside him.

"Do you see that?" Bill asked, and Jake looked toward where he was pointing. A few black dots seemed to move in front of them, but he couldn't tell if they were animals or humans. "Stay quiet and don't move," Bill said. Jake slowed his breath even though no one would be able to hear it. "Get down, and close your ears!" Bill ordered.

"What?" Jake saw Bill take something out of his saddlebag, and attend to both of the horses.

"Flash bomb! Get down!"

Jake fell to the ground.

Bang! Jake couldn't move for a second, and when he came to, he saw blurry figures running toward them. Someone picked him up and shook him.

"Jake!" Bill slapped his face. "Take this." He handed him a .45 caliber.

Still disoriented, Jake pointed the gun at the advancing figures. Both of their horses were lying on the ground. "I think they're shooting!" Jake screamed. He pressed the trigger, but nothing came out.

"Take the safety off!" Bill shouted, but when Jake didn't move, he did it for him. Bill stood next to Jake, holding his pistol, aiming.

"Why aren't you shooting? They have guns!" Jake cried out and watched as bullets flew by them. One bounced off Jake's arm and it hurt, but no blood came out. *What the hell?* He started shooting. By the time he realized he was off target, Bill had shot off two rounds and hit two of the perpetrators—both in the legs.

The rest of the assailants got closer, three men led by a woman. They all wore piecemeal jackets and dirty jeans. The men were lanky, and the woman, shorter than most, had a protruding belly.

Jake noticed Bill lowering his gun. "What are you doing?" he whispered. "We need to defend ourselves!"

Bill pointed at the woman's stomach.

"Let's make this simple for everyone." Three feet away, the woman spoke in a raspy voice. "Give us your goods and we'll be on our way."

"I don't think so," Bill said. "Your rubber pellets won't kill us, but our bullets will kill you." Bill gestured at the two men lying on the ground, screeching in pain.

Jake saw understanding enter the woman's eyes. He wasn't sure, but it seemed her pupils were growing large and then small again, large and small—a side effect of volt.

"Real bullets, eh?" she said and spat. Her mouth had sores, her face was pocked, but Jake could tell she was once pretty.

"It's your move," Bill said. One of the men leaped toward them, but before Jake could fire a shot, the man was down from Bill's bullet, writhing in pain.

"You are good with that gun," the woman said. "Why don't you ride with us? We have good money coming in. I'll make it worth your while." She winked at Bill, her eyes dilating and contracting, dilating and contracting.

"Why don't you go your separate way," Bill said.

"You're missing a good ride, cowboy." She moved backward, gyrating her hips and staring at them wide-eyed. "C'mon boys, let's get out of here."

Bill took the gun from Jake and put it back in his holster. "What the hell was that? Volters?"

"Yes, volters. A lot of them around here, but I've never seen them so forward."

"I figured by the eyes," Jake said, and cocked his head. "You shot like three of them. How did you do that?"

"We should set up camp," Bill said, ignoring the question.

"Here?" Jake looked at the volters walking away.

"I gave the horses tranquilizers so they wouldn't run when the flash bomb went off."

Jake looked at Delight sitting down, her front legs tucked beneath the breast, drooling, eyes glazed over. Morpheus sat next to her in a similar fashion, twitching once in a while as his body tried to break through the sedative constraint.

"It will take a few hours before the drug wears off and it will be dark by then," Bill explained.

"What about the volters?"

"They won't be back, and they'll tell their friends to stay away."

~ ~ ~

"So, um"—Jake cleared his throat—"where did you learn how to shoot like that?" he asked as they sat by the fire, hours later. "Did you, um, train in the military or something?"

"Military?" Bill put down his utensils, his expression carried a hint of uneasiness.

"Not just because of the shooting. The military pouches we eat . . ." Jake scooped a forkful of a gooey mess that tasted like beef and rice.

Bill squinted his eyes but didn't say anything.

Jake started to feel uncomfortable, but pushed on anyway. "The pre-dawn exercise routine is also a bit of a giveaway."

Bill looked off to the side. "Yes, I trained."

"I knew it! What sort of training was it?" Jake asked, food still in his mouth.

"It's not a part of my past I like to remember. It happened right after Emmy—I was in a dark place and they were in the right place, at the right time. Convinced me it was what I needed."

"What type of stuff did you do? Anything I can hear about?"

Bill shook his head. "I'd rather not."

"Just one story?" Jake looked around. "Doesn't look like anyone's listening."

"It was a long time ago," Bill said.

"Was it dangerous? Did you ever have to kill anyone?" Jake popped off the questions, curiosity getting the best of him.

Bill furrowed his brow, but didn't say anything.

"Come on, we've been traveling together for months now, you can trust me."

Bill wiped his mouth with a napkin and tossed it into the flames. "The first assignment is always the hardest," he said, looking down at the ground.

September 2047 ~ 13 Years Ago
Bill Vos – Metropolitans
San Francisco, California

Alex White was the name of the man Bill was ordered to extract information from. A Russian mobster, known for selling volt and sex-trafficking. The assignment was simple enough: find the man, interrogate the man, kill the man. *How did I end up here?* Bill thought.

He sat in his government provided San Francisco apartment, cleaning his gun. I'm going to torture and kill a man, he thought. That's what they trained me for, and that's what I need to do.

He put his gun away, and began re-adjusting a spy scope he had set up to look into the condo across the street; this is where Alex White lived with his wife and two young daughters. Watching their day to day lives was like watching a television show. The image in the scope cleared up and focused on White's wife. She was tall, blond and blue-eyed; her features honed a natural beauty. Today, she was wearing stiletto heels, jeans and a leather jacket. Emmy had a similar jacket, but Emmy's had more character. She wore it every single day, each tear—each scratch—a memory. *God, I miss you Emmy.* Bill sighed, then moved over to his black suitcase and pulled out the listening equipment.

For months, Bill observed Alex White. He seemed so normal—so routine. White would wake up at six in the morning each day, his wife would cook porridge and fruit; a family breakfast followed by school drop-offs and work. Bill took detailed notes of each family member's coming and going. The wife, it turned out, was cheating on Alex with his bodyguard. White knew, but didn't seem to care. The more Bill watched, the harder it was for him to imagine how he would kill the father of this family, leaving a mother and two kids behind. Nonetheless, he knew he had to finish the job.

When Bill felt he was ready, he made his move. He dressed himself in a black baseball hat, shirt, pants, and boots all covered with a thin layer of ad blinder, a film which made him invisible to all ad sensors. He followed White, intercepting him at the gas station where White bought his daily pack of cigarettes. As soon as White walked away, Bill hacked into his self-driving car to unlock the passenger door. He crouched in the front seat until White came back in. When White sat down, Bill recalibrated the locks to remain closed and overrode White's mapped route; the new route took them to an abandoned warehouse.

It was a quiet ride with Bill's gun pointed at White through the space between the front seats. The first hour they spent on a highway, and the second hour, on a dirt road. The warehouse, although far from populated areas, was equipped with an ad detractor, which created an illusion that all of the warehouse ad real estate was bought out. This way, there would be no surprises from opportunistic ad buyers.

"You going to kill me?" The mobster asked, but his gray eyes held no fear.

"Perhaps," Bill lied.

"I won't talk. You might as well kill me now."

"Well, I'm here to make sure you do talk," Bill said, pointing to a box of tools.

White grimaced.

"I just need a place and name. The shipping container with the girls, and the name of the man on other end."

"If I give you that name, I'm as good as dead." Alex shrugged.

"Yes, but think of your family." Bill took a picture out of his pocket. It was a picture of White's last birthday; the family sat at a secluded table in an expensive Italian restaurant, all wearing fake, bleached-teeth smiles.

White's nostril's flared. "Leave my family out of this."

"That will be up to you," Bill said, taking out a razor.

"Name." Bill brought the tool close enough to White's neck to draw a thin line of blood.

White spat on the floor.

"Shame." Bill put the razor down, deciding to take a different approach. He unwrapped the rest of his tools, picking out a pair of pliers. He ripped off White's fingernails, watching the nailbeds fill with blood as jagged chunks of keratin fell on the floor. White began to breathe uneasily and a film of moisture covered his skin. He didn't talk. Bill needed to press on.

Crack! Bill broke White's pinky finger. He felt the bones separate through his glove. White didn't talk. *Crack!* This time it was his pointer. Still nothing. *Crack!* White shivered at the break of his middle finger, but still not a word. *Crack!* White's body jerked. I'm getting close, Bill thought.

"Tell me," Bill demanded.

Alex spat, this time in Bill's face. Bill wiped the slime with his glove, and stayed quiet. He decided to turn his attention to White's other hand. *Slice.* He cut through White's thumb, leaving a little skin to let the digit dangle. White gagged; his body was drenched in sweat. Still not a word. *Slice.* Half-digested breakfast spilled out of White's mouth onto the floor. *Slice.* A scream escaped. *Slice.* Drops of piss stained the floor. It took half an hour and seven digits before the name rolled off White's tongue. Now, he sat defeated; blood dripped freely from him, onto a plastic tarp underneath.

"That's all I needed," Bill said, disturbed by how little the process had affected him. It was as if he wasn't there, torturing a man.

"Tell me, am I going to die?" White interrupted Bill's thoughts.

"Yes."

"Can I ask you for a favor?"

"No."

"Please. I want to say goodbye to my family. Can you write a note to my wife and my kids?"

Protocol did not allow this, but it would give the family closure. Something Bill had never got with Emmy. "Okay," he said.

"Please write down: I love you very much and will miss you dearly. I had to disappear. For your own safety, I don't know if I will be able to contact you anymore. You are everything to me. Stay strong, stay safe, and make your mother proud."

Bill wrote down the message on a piece of paper, folded it, and put it in his pocket. He took out his silencer. "You ready?" he asked.

White nodded.

One shot to the back of the head and it was over. After everything he did to White, it was the sound of the bullet hitting flesh that made Bill feel sick to his stomach. He wanted to vomit, but held it in—no DNA at the crime scene.

The adrenaline that had run through him made the memories of the cleanup hazy. Later that night, when he was back in his government issued apartment, he looked at himself in the mirror, and did not recognize the man looking back at him.

December 2060 – Present Day
Bill Vos – The Red Rocks
Road to Manti, Utah

Bill took a drink, the water tasted sour as if the memories had soaked themselves in it. He looked at Jake, who sat hanging on every word, chain smoking his rolled cigarettes.

"Did . . . did you drop off the note?" Jake asked.

"What?" Bill was deep in thought and then realized what Jake meant. The kid wants to see my true colors, he thought. Smart. He shook his head back and forth, then said, "I did."

Jake nodded. "You're a good man for doing that."

"I'm not so sure," Bill said, remorse in his voice. He looked down at his hand and realized he had been holding Emmy's ring throughout the story, flipping it from one side to the other.

"Good, means you protect your country and that's what you did."

"But that means nothing if you can't protect the ones you love." Bill put the ring in his pocket.

After a moment of quiet, Jake asked, "What was this military position anyway? It doesn't sound like anything normal."

"We were an internal black ops group, created and hired by the government for the military. I found out that the group was going to be dismantled. There are stories about groups that get dismantled. The military doesn't like to have liabilities—leave loose ends. That's why I came to the Red Rocks."

Jake nodded. "That's intense. What else—"

"That's enough for today. Time to go to bed," Bill stated, and, although he had told Jake the volters wouldn't come back, he knew he would have to stay awake to make sure.

December 2060 – Present Day
Jake Deen – The Red Rocks
Road to Livingsworth, Nevada

Bang! The bottle Jake was aiming at shook, but did not fall off of the tree stump.

"Lean over to the left," Bill said, and adjusted Jake's shoulders. Bill had said that Jake needed the practice after seeing him handle the volters. It was a good day for shooting—no wind, brisk air.

Jake pictured Anna's client Sebastián as he aimed at his target. Damn bastard, he doesn't deserve to be with her, only I do, he thought.

Bang! He missed again and went to get more bullets.

"If you are shooting someone to slow them down, try for the legs," Bill lectured. "If you are shooting to kill, try for the head. If that's not good, then two to the chest. The latter is always the safest bet. Bigger target area."

Bang! This time he got it! "Yes! First one down!" He jumped up in celebration.

"First, but not the last," Bill said. "Here." He picked up a casing next to Jake's foot. "It's the one from your good shot. Something to remember this moment by."

Jake picked up the tiny gold cylinder proudly. He rolled it in his hand feeling the dents, a tiny cross was etched into the flattened back. Jake tucked the casing away safely in his pocket, thankful for this day. Thankful for Anna. Thankful for Bill. Thankful for Bobby. He didn't need anyone else. He didn't need his father.

Jake looked at Bill, who had let his hair down; Jake hadn't realized how long it had gotten, running down past his shoulders. It was mostly gray now. Bill is a good man, Jake thought. It is hard to believe he has such a dark past. Jake saw him as a man of high standards. A man of solid morals. I guess you never really know someone, he thought. One thing he did know, is that Bill was a good man to keep close.

"Hey Bill. Do you want to come and have dinner sometime? You can meet my girl . . . ahem . . . my friend."

Bill looked at him, deep in thought. "I appreciate your offer, Jake. But I think your"—Bill paused—"friend, would find me uninteresting."

"Come on, it will be a good time," Jake said. "She's not like anyone else. I think you two would get along well."

Bill stayed quiet.

"She's a wonderful cook. What's your favorite meal, steak? She always gets it to a perfect medium-rare, and her mashed potatoes—I don't know what she does but they are the creamiest I've ever had and—"

"Thank you, but not at this time," Bill said.

That was a quick no, Jake thought. He felt a little hurt. He wanted to ask why, but decided against it and emptied the rest of his clip shattering three bottles.

December 2060 – Present Day
Anna Faroe – The Red Rocks
Livingsworth, Nevada

Anna brushed a warm washcloth over Jake's shoulder and droplets ran down, becoming one with the discolored water in the marble tub. The scent of cinnamon and nutmeg wafted through the air. Anna was glad to see him after two weeks of him being away. "Tell me more about your adventures on the road," she said.

Jake's eyes popped open with excitement. "You won't believe what happened!" He told Anna about the volters springing up on them.

Anna rubbed fragrant soap onto the cloth and scrubbed Jake's muscular back. "Tell me about your riding partner. He seems knowledgeable." *And dangerous.*

"He's experienced," Jake said. "And we travel well together."

Anna waited for Jake to continue, but he didn't. Interesting. No need to pry. He will tell me when he is ready, she thought. "I'm glad you're safe." Anna brought her fingers to his chin and pulled him in for a kiss.

"I'm glad I'm here." Jake nuzzled her neck. Anna giggled, pulling away and gave him a playful splash.

"How long are you in town for? Do you know?" she asked. She hoped it would be as long as last time.

Jake shook his head. "Bill didn't give me a schedule for our next ride. He said he'd send notice to Bobby." Jake looked into her eyes. "But I know I'm spending every free moment I have, with you."

Anna swirled the foamy water with her finger. "Have you given more thought about meeting with your father?" She looked up at him.

Jake turned away. "I tried to keep him out my head for now."

Anna knew he was being honest. She also knew there was no way Jake could get his father out of his head. No one would be able to—not with the relationship they had. "I have a feeling he will come find you again. I want you to know that I support you no matter what decision you make."

"I know," Jake said. "That's why I wanted to ask you something."

Anna felt what he wanted to ask.

He got up and she wrapped a soft white robe around him. They made their way to the bedroom which was decorated with mistletoe and poinsettia plants. Anna sat down on the bed, her satin shorts riding up her thighs.

"I"—Jake cleared his throat—"I've been thinking a lot about it, and I don't want you to keep clients anymore."

Anna shifted her weight and brushed her fingers through her thick dark strands. "Jake I—"

"No, please listen. We can be together." Jake walked over to her side of the bed and knelt, holding her hands in his. "What we have here is real. It can grow. I know you see it too."

Anna sighed and looked away.

"Please give us a chance to be together. I will do anything you want."

Anna tried to move away, but Jake pulled her back.

"Anna, the way I feel about you, it's like movie love. I know you feel the same way too. And . . . and if you realize that you don't like this, if you don't want it to be just me or if you want to help people, we can go back to the way things were," Jake persuaded.

Was she ready? Anna sat for a few moments, quiet. Jake massaged her hands with his thumbs. "Okay," she said finally, knowing that the option to go back to the way things were, was not really option.

December 2060 – Present Day
Jake Deen – The Red Rocks
Livingsworth, Nevada

"Checkmate!" Bobby yelled as Jake came through the door a few days later. He was carrying a box of margarita mix.

"The main store just got their government supply drop, so I picked these up for the holiday party. The line was out the door, but the owner kept these especially for you." Jake grinned.

"I requested that a half a year ago. I guess luck is in my favor today," Bobby said, gesturing to the chessboard; his opponent got up and muttered under his breath. "Don't be a sore loser. I'll give you a chance to win it back next time." Bobby smiled and turned his attention back to Jake.

"I got you the battery cassette recorder." Jake moved the compact case with two reels and magnetic tape across the bar.

"Thanks. This will help me out a lot. By the way, you have a visitor here. He's been coming in, looking for you the last couple of days." Bobby smoothed out his mustache and nodded toward the back of the bar.

"Jake!" a familiar voice called out.

Jake turned around and saw his father exiting the restroom, zipping up his fly.

"What are you doing here?" Jake said through his teeth.

"You never came to see me, so I thought I'd check in on you, in case you lost my address."

"I never took your address. How did you find me?"

"You mentioned you never made it to Livingsworth until now. I was going up this way anyhow; decided to stay an extra day or so to see if I could find ya."

Jake took notice of David's slurred speech, ill smell, and liquor-stained clothes. He was wearing the same thing he wore when they ran into each other in Goldfield.

"I even tried to get the bartender here to tell me where you're stayin', but he said he don't know."

Jake mouthed a silent "thank you" to Bobby, who responded with a nod.

"Do you have some time to spend with your ol' man?"

"I have to work," Jake said.

"Oh," David said, his face falling.

Jake slammed the box of margarita mix down on the bar. *Why does he think he can just come back into my life and everything will be okay?*

David sighed. "Well, I wanted to let you know that I found your mom's old journal. Her mother sent it to me after 8/6/2040, along with several other belongings. I thought you might want to read it."

"Can't you just leave it with me?"

David frowned. "I don't have it with me, Son. It's at my hotel. I was hoping we can go through it together."

"I'd rather not. Can you go get it and bring it to me?"

"Jake . . . you know I—"

"I don't want to hear it," Jake interrupted. He knew the "Jake . . . you know I" speech all too well. He exhaled loudly in frustration. "I have to work, but I'll meet you in a couple hours." Jake didn't want his father around his friends. He didn't want him back in his life, erasing the anger, the years of pain and abandonment. "We'll meet at your place. Where are you staying?" Jake asked.

David's face exerted joy, and he went in for hug that Jake did not reciprocate.

December 2060 – Present Day
Bill Vos – The Red Rocks
Kingman, Nevada

"I have a different kind of errand for you," said Tommy, and picked up a cigar, chewed off the end, and spat it on the floor. Bill had come over to give an update on his last run. Now, hearing this, Bill tensed up.

"There is a man I have a problem with. I've talked to this man several times about getting my money, and nothing." Tommy's belly bulged out from beneath his jacket as leaned back in his oversized office chair. "You see," Tommy started, "there are necessary means to having your bank survive in The Red Rocks. For one, you need to be able to get people to pay you back."

"So what do you want me to do?" Bill asked.

The greasy man pretended to look deep in thought, then took off his glasses and put them on the desk.

"Well, I can't have this happening anymore. Not with him," he said.

The history with the man in question was a very long one. He had owed Tommy money on and off for years. This time the sum was large, and the man hadn't paid Tommy a penny in one year. Bill sensed there was personal anger as well; rumors suggested that Tommy's whore liked another man, perhaps this was him.

"I chose you, Bill, because this time, a simple talking to just won't work," Tommy said. "And because you owe me a favor."

Bill cleared his throat. "What exactly are you asking me?"

"You know." Tommy took an inhale of peppery smoke and blew it toward Bill's face.

"And if we get caught?"

Tommy slammed his palm on the table. "Don't play dumb with me, Bill. You think I don't know what you've done?" He scoffed. "Remember the man who introduced us—the man who got you to the Red Rocks. He is *my* friend, not yours." Tommy walked out from behind the desk and sat on it, staring Bill in the face. "I know what you are capable of. But if you fuck up"—he blew another round of smoke in Bill's face—"you know what *I* am capable of."

Bill's hand wrapped around his gun. "Tell me how the surgery went."

Confusion flashed on Tommy's face. "What?" Bill took his gun out and placed the barrel to Tommy's crotch. "The surgery for my mother-in-law. How. Did. It. Go?"

Tommy coughed. "It went well. I"—Tommy's forehead exuded liquid—"I have the medical reports."

"Get them." Bill tighten the grip on his gun, and Tommy rushed to his desk. Bill pressed his finger slightly further into the trigger, knowing that the drawer Tommy had opened was the one where he kept his revolver. A moment later, Bill was glad to see Tommy pull out a red folder and hand it to him.

Bill looked over the papers.

"The surgery went okay, but she's in intensive care after catching pneumonia. She needs medication." Tommy's voice shook as he spoke. "I can keep her there until she recovers as long as you do what I ask."

"Fine, but I'll need papers for every day she's in the hospital, and I'll need payment. Double of my last run."

Tommy cringed. "Papers and one and a half."

Bill nodded. He hated himself for agreeing. It had been a long time since he's done a job like this.

December 2060 – Present Day
Jake Deen – The Red Rocks
Livingsworth, Nevada

Jake stayed at Bobby's a few hours longer than he planned, rattled by David's sudden visit. Work calmed him down, and after he felt his anxiety subside, he went to meet up with David at his hotel. The place was small and funky. The walls were painted neon, and the bartender wore an oversized, off-the-shoulder shirt with her hair done into a side ponytail. She bounced around to a 1980s greatest hits album while she poured cocktails.

"You want a drink, Son?" David had changed into clean jeans and combed his white hair over to one side, in an attempt to hide the baldness.

Jake reviewed the options on the bar shelves, and then said, "Club soda, if you have it." He had acquired a taste for the drink.

"No liquor, huh? That's good. It's okay if I do?"

Jake smirked. "You're a shitty parent anyway. Go ahead."

"Jake, I just want you to know that I loved you and I tried my best," David said.

"Doesn't look like your best was good enough." Jake shifted in his seat, feeling a familiar anger.

"Right." David sighed. "You forget that you were no piece of cake to deal with. You were a wild child. I tried grounding, I tried to put you in therapy, I tried everything I could. I had to send you away because it wasn't safe anymore."

"What are you taking about?" Jake rolled his eyes—he remembered it drove David crazy when he was a teenager.

David didn't pay attention. He looked through Jake, his gaze drifting to a different time. "Once, you threw a party at the house. I was out for the night, and when I came back you were passed out on the bathroom floor and half of our stuff was gone: our TV, my golf clubs, your mom's jewelry . . ."

Don't remember that party, Jake thought, a bit embarrassed—not because of the party, but because of his mom's jewelry.

"Anyway, when you came to, you said that there was no party, and that an Asian gang stormed the house and robbed us." David laughed.

"I bet you beat the hell out of me after. Nothing to be laughing about," Jake fumed.

David's face sank. "No, Son. I did not hit you. Not that night."

Fucker.

David looked away. He swallowed the contents of his mug and ordered another. His veiny hands shook.

Jake pushed away his drink. "We're done here. Where is the journal?"

David took it out of his jacket pocket and slid it over to Jake, who took it and got up to leave.

"Won't you stay with me a little longer?"

"I don't think so."

"Jake I would really love it if you did. Don't you want to go through it together? Please?"

"No." Jake threw down a Red Rock note and left.

December 2060 – Present Day
Anna Faroe – The Red Rocks
Livingsworth, Nevada

Anna, her lips stained from her favorite merlot, watched the last page of her client book burn in a pit in her backyard. She stood up and poured the last bit of wine in her glass onto the licks of flame. The wind picked up making her dress cling against her skin, and she stared off into the distance. She could see a faint future of her and Jake growing old together.

Knock. Knock. Anna walked in and opened the door.

"Anna, please, just give me one more session!" Adrian Almante, one of her clients, stood in an unwashed shirt and pants from days spent at the bar. Tall, thin, and with pleading eyes, he looked like a lost child.

"I can't, I told you." Anna felt sorry for him. She knew he had no other family or friends.

"I just want to talk," Adrian pleaded and pushed his way in. Anna backed away.

"You know our time will always be special, but I'm with someone now. I'm changing my life and you have to respect that."

"Who is this bastard? I can change your life. I want to stay with you forever too!"

"It's not up to you. I am my own woman," Anna said. *I am.*

"What does he have that I don't?" Adrian looked from side to side. "I am all the man you need!" He flipped over her coffee table. Two tea cups smashed onto the floor. Then he pushed her up against the wall, and pressed against her.

"Adrian, stop!"

He fell to his knees and kissed her feet. Then he hugged her and she looked down on him.

She petted his head. "This is what I want."

January 2061 – Present Day
Jake Deen – The Red Rocks
Livingsworth, Nevada

Jake sat in Anna's bedroom, one month later, looking at his Mom's journal. He hadn't opened it. He was waiting for the right moment. Today would've been her sixty-fifth birthday. *Am I ready to see this?* he thought. He wasn't sure he wanted to. He felt scared, like she must've felt. Jake lit a cigarette. *All I have is this memory of her. I have to see, no matter if it's good or bad. Mom, why did you leave this world so soon?*

March 2040 ~ 21 Years Ago
Sandra Deen – Metropolitans
Outskirts of San Francisco, California

Sandra stood, looking out into a purple field of flowers. *I miss you Jack*, she thought. *Wait, is it Jack or Jake? Or is it Jax?* I tear rolled down her cheek. Her mind wanted to remember, but it couldn't. She was in a field of purple flowers, that's all she knew. Their soft petals tickled her legs and their perfume flooded her nostrils. *Bam!* She wasn't in a field at all, but standing in a supermarket. The field was hologram commercial for lavender soap which lay in front of her, urging her to make a purchase. She ran out of the store. Or did she?

She took out a piece of paper, the publication she signed up for, and reviewed the date and time.

> August 6th, 2040. We will stand together in resistance to this malicious world full of falsehood.

She sat down in the fake grass. She didn't know how, but she knew it was fake. I love you so much Jax, Jake, Jack? I wish I could see you again. I wish I could. I wish I could. But this is the right way. David. I miss him too. David? No, not David. Well, David too. I guess.

She looked around, she was in a car going somewhere. The seats were comforting, and it smelled of leather, or of suede, or silk? She forgot the right scent reference. I'm going to see you one more time before I go, she thought.

"What did you think? A computer screen appeared in front of her. She wasn't in a car at all. She didn't know where she was. "Stop!!!" she screamed. She crumpled to the floor, what floor, she didn't know, and closed her eyes.

I love you dearly, whatever your name is. My mind now cannot comprehend. In one reality it's Jack, in one it's Jax, in one it's Jake. I can no longer tell the real world apart from the fake.

A lady popped up next to me yesterday, I wasn't sure if she was real, but she told me you were Jack, but I don't think that's your name. You are a teen, and you are a boy, maybe it's Jake? No, that doesn't sound right either.

Whoever you are, I just want you to know Jack, no, Jake, no . . . whoever! If you ever read this, but how can you read this if I don't know your name? But if you do read this, all I want you to know, is that I love you. And wherever you are, please forgive me for what I have to do. I hope your father can bring you comfort. He is a good man, and I hope you two will get along. My biggest hope is that you two are close. You can make it through anything together.

Sandra hadn't realized, but she was writing everything down in a little blue journal.

January 2061 – Present Day
Jake Deen – The Red Rocks
Livingsworth, Nevada

Jake was standing outside of David's new hotel a week later. He noticed David didn't like staying in one place for longer than a few days. Overrunning his tab, or his welcome, or both, Jake guessed. *I could leave right now, I could, but this is what Mom would've wanted.* He went in and found David at the bar. The hotel was decorated with disco balls and peace signs; thin lines of smoke penetrated the room now and again, leaving a thick herbal scent.

"Jake! I knew you'd come." David motioned for him to come over. "A round of non-alcoholic beverages on me." Jake could tell David was already tipsy. He appreciated David's gesture not to drink in front of him.

The bartender rolled his eyes. "Water then?"

"Yes," Jake said as he sat down on a puffy stool. "Are there more journals?"

David shook his head, sadness swimming in his eyes. "No, this is the only one I have."

Jake's water arrived and he drank the lukewarm liquid. "She was in a lot of pain," he said.

"I know, son, but she was an amazing woman who loved you very much." David smiled. "Do you remember that you, your mom, and I used to go out fishing almost every month? We found a little secret spot with the best view of the lake," David said and sipped his cup of water. Jake saw him cringe at the unfamiliar taste.

"I remember." Jake nodded and recalled when he'd cast his line out for the first time, his mom sitting next to him atop a quilt she had made from his baby pictures.

"You didn't use any of those special smartphone rods that lured the fish, you used an old-fashioned one. When we came down to the main beach with three bass and two trout, the other fishermen were green with envy." David laughed.

"She was so happy." Jake leaned back on his plush, pink bar stool. *She was so proud.*

"She was . . . then." David brushed his thinning hair to one side, covering his baldness. "She was always surrounded by people. Her beauty and wit drew you in. She had so much love, to give, and she loved you more than anything else in this world. You."

"I know." Jake smiled a sad smile.

"I remember we also used to go—all three of us—for walks to pick mushrooms. When we'd come home, your mom would marinate them, and we'd eat your favorite lunch—cucumber and cream cheese sandwiches. God you loved those sandwiches. Wouldn't eat nothin' else for a whole three months one time, we had to ween you off them." David chuckled.

Jake's mouth watered at the memory. For a second, he felt the presence of his mother's love. "I miss her."

"I miss her too, Son."

February 2061 – Present Day
Anna Faroe – The Red Rocks
Livingsworth, Nevada

Anna set the square kitchen table for three. She wore a flowy dress colored with pink and green hummingbirds. The aroma of rosemary and garlic hung in the air.

"Are you sure about this?" Anna asked, taking Jake's hands in hers. He looked different from when she first met him—stronger. Jake had invited David for dinner, and she was worried about him getting too close. She didn't like the man from what she knew of him, and wasn't sure she wanted him in her or Jake's life.

"I know you're skeptical, but I think that my mom would've wanted this. I'm doing it for her." Jake kissed Anna's forehead. "Plus, he's been around for the last few weeks and he seems to want to get to know me."

He wasn't going to listen, but she needed to tell him how she felt. "It's your decision, of course, but I have to tell you that I don't trust him. The story of him sending you away still doesn't make sense to me. I feel like he's hiding something."

"I trust you Anna, and your intuition, but I want to try to have a relationship with him. If I get hurt, then I get hurt. For me, the memories of childhood that he's surfaced, the memories of my mom, they make me feel closer to her, and that makes it worth any future pain." Jake squeezed Anna tight and moved his hand up and down her back.

"Okay," Anna said. "If this is what you want, then I support it."

"I would've never had the strength to do this without you. You changed me." Jake held her close.

"You changed on your own, Jake."

"I love you, Anna."

"I love you too." She smiled, but worry dabbed at her heart.

February 2061 – Present Day
Jake Deen – The Red Rocks
Livingsworth, Nevada

An hour later, Jake sat on the same side as Anna at the table, across from David. Mashed potatoes, collard greens, fresh rolls and a pork roast stood on the table, steaming. It smelled like every family home should.

"David, tell me. What is your life like in Goldfield?" Anna asked and took a bite of her slice of meat.

"I get by," David said. He didn't elaborate.

"Have you always lived there?"

"No, I moved around for a while." David crunched down on a toasty roll.

"And what about now? Will you be moving?" Anna's lips held a straight line. Jake didn't see curiosity, only judgement.

"I'm not planning to move anytime soon. Why do you ask?" David looked up at her, but quickly looked away.

"I want to make sure we are aware of your intentions," Anna said, her voice stern. "If you are to stay in our lives, we need you to be honest and direct."

Jake put his hand on hers and squeezed it. He liked that she was worried about him.

David patted down the combed-over hair on his head, and worry flashed on his face. "I don't understand what you mean. Is there anything specific you think I'm keeping from you?"

"Do *you* think there is?" Anna asked.

David drank a pull of his water. "Anna, I can assure you that there is nothing more important to me in this world than to have this relationship. I promise that I will tell you anything you want or need to know."

"Okay," Anna said, but did not seem convinced. They finished the rest of dinner in a silence broken only by a word here or there to complement Anna's cooking.

After they finished eating, Jake and David sat on the back porch, smoking their after-dinner cigars and watching the sunset.

"You have one beautiful and smart woman there." David's eyes wandered over to the kitchen window, where Anna, hair pulled back, was washing dishes in the basin.

"I know." Jake blew out rings of smoke and took a sip of his iced tea.

"So why the sudden change of heart? I know you didn't want me to meet Anna at first."

Jake looked off to the side.

"It's getting serious between you two," David conversed with himself out loud. "You're thinking about asking her to marry you, aren't you?"

Jake gave a slight nod.

"Oh, Son." David put his cigar out and patted Jake on the shoulder. "I can tell from the way you look at her that you love her. It's the same way I used to look at your mother."

Jake put out his own cigar and rubbed his hands nervously on his thighs. "You know, I never thought I'd get here."

"And where is that?" David asked.

"Being happy, having a home. It never crossed my mind that this was an option for me." The temperature dropped several degrees as the sun made its descent. Jake pulled his sweater closer around him.

"I felt the same way before I met your mother. She made me a better man—she made me happy."

Jake nodded and stared out into the distance watching clouds roll over the mountains in an apocalyptic wave.

"You know, I still have your mother's ring."

"Mom." Jake smiled as he remembered the way she used to tousle his hair.

"You should take a trip up to Goldfield and I will give it to you."

"Okay," Jake agreed. Is it me, he thought, or is David finally starting to act like a real father?

February 2061 – Present Day
Bill Vos – The Red Rocks
Wells, Nevada

Bill sat on his skillfully made bed, every sheet-corner and fold—a perfect angle. He looked at the list in his hand: pistol, knife, rope, horseshoes, kerosene (for the lamp), water, jerky, Red Rocks pellets, salt packets, towel. Every item was crossed out, except horseshoes. He'd need to pick up some new ones up.

Bill organized his supplies to fit into his leather travel sack. Next, he pulled out the same black metal box he looked at every time he was at home. He moved the stack of money and passports out of the way, and took out a silencer. Old enemy, old friend, he thought. He ran his fingers over the surface, attached it to his gun, and aimed it at the wall. Then, he took out the envelope Tommy had handed him. Bill had avoided looking inside, at times wondering if he should burn it, ride away, and never come back to this part of the Red Rocks. But he couldn't do that to Emmy. He'd made her a promise that he would take care of her family, and right now, he needed Tommy to keep his promise, to get his mother-in-law the treatment she needed.

He sighed and looked at the ceiling. Time was running out. The mark was not a good man, after all. He tried to rationalize with himself as he fingered the manila sleeve. But if he did this, he would be going back to what he had ran away from.

He opened the flap. There is no other way, he thought, then he pulled out the photograph inside the envelope. He couldn't believe it. He shook with anger. *It must be fate.*

December 2050 ~ 11 Years Ago
Bill Vos – Metropolitans
San Francisco, California

A felon stood in front of Bill, a man who was not supposed to live. Bill was ordered to kill this man, but instead he made a deal—intel for a new identity and transport to the Red Rocks. He didn't want to risk finding out what the military would do after they dismantled his black ops team; this was his way out.

The large silver-haired man handed Bill a stack of money, a few domestic and foreign passports, and a few contacts in the Red Rocks. This is it, he thought, no turning back.

"You made a wise decision my friend," the man said, in his thick Eastern European accent. The man had always made a point that Bill was doing the right thing by coming to him instead of following his employer's orders.

"Perhaps," Bill said, his face blank, his soul empty.

"Your own people would have killed you after they were done using you to do their dirty work." The man spat. "No loyalty."

"Loyalty is hard to come by these days," Bill responded.

The man grinned, the light from the lamp reflecting off of his gold teeth.

"You're a smart man, Bill. And as a token of our appreciation, here is something for you." The man threw down a packet in front of him. "Call it a going-away present."

Bill opened it up to find a prison release form.

"What's this?"

He pulled out the second piece of paper. It was a black and white photo of a face that was forever etched in his mind.

"The man who killed your wife. He's out."

February 2061 – Present Day
Jake Deen – The Red Rocks
Goldfield, Nevada

Jake made good time on his journey to Goldfield. He was barely able to push through the crowd on the street that led to his father's hotel. People had gathered to watch as two men wearing cowboy hats drew and shot at each with fake guns. They were reluctant to budge for him and Delight. I wonder why he's staying in a hotel, Jake thought as he looked for the right address. Maybe he's embarrassed of where he lives, or maybe something else is going on. He does seem to be traveling a lot.

After thirty minutes, Jake found the hotel. It was small and weathered. As soon as he walked in, he was hit with a smell of cigarettes and cheap perfume. His father sat at the lacquered bar, chatting with a middle-aged woman.

"Jake!" His father waved him over, excitement in his milky eyes. "I'm glad you could come."

Jake walked over and patted David on the back. He was wearing his black velvet jacket and his hair, or lack thereof, was in its usual combed-over state.

"It isn't the greatest town in the world, being small and touristy, but it's my home now."

"The feeling of home—it's something special," Jake commented. He felt balanced. He felt good.

"It is, and I can tell you're starting to think of Livingsworth as yours."

"I am." Jake took off his checkered sweater and sat down.

"I'm really happy for you, Son." David signaled the bartender to bring them two waters, after gulping down the rest of his beer. He turned to Jake. "I like Anna, and I know your mom would like her too. She would be happy to know that her ring will go to the woman you love. A woman who takes care of you," he said.

"Do you have the ring with you?"

"No, it's at my place. Before I give it to you, I want to tell you something. I wasn't sure if I should, but I think it's best that you and Anna know the truth."

Jake recalled Anna's comment about David hiding something. "Tell me then."

"Not here. Not today. I have a day planned for us tomorrow. We're going to have a nice brunch, go for a ride, and then we'll get the ring. I also have some money saved up I'd like to give you for the wedding. I'd like to tell you then."

"Really?"

"Jake . . . you know I—"

"Why even tell me this if you're going to make me wait?" Jake asked in frustration.

"I just want you to be in a good place when I tell you. It's important. Right now you're tired."

"You're playing your games again—the secrets and excuses. Just be straight with me for once."

"You're right, I shouldn't have said anything. I'm sorry." David looked down.

"It's okay, Dad." Jake's mouth curved down as soon as the words came out. He saw David smile and his eyes water. The child inside him felt a certain peace, but a part of him was mad at himself for saying the words. He wasn't sure if he was ready to deal with his subconscious accepting his father to the point of calling him 'dad' again. All of sudden, he felt really tired.

He finished his water. "I'm exhausted from the trip. I think it's best if I turn in."

"Okay, Son." David motioned for the bartender to bring him something stronger. "I love you. I think your mom would be happy to see us spending time together."

February 2061 – Present Day
Jake Deen – The Red Rocks
Goldfield, Nevada

Jake woke up at dawn, his muscles sore from the ride, his belly empty. He took his waterskin and chugged the remains. The cold stale coffee inside tasted like dirt, but it woke him up. It was early, but he should go see if his dad was awake. He knew his dad liked his breakfast shots, although at this time, he doubted the bar was open.

Jake washed his face, shaved, and pulled his blond hair back into a ponytail. He'd deal with brushing that later. He pulled on a clean pair of jeans and a T-shirt, excited to start the day—the day he will never forget.

Bang! A gun shot rang out followed by the sound of shattering glass.

Jake edged toward his door. *Bang!* He made his way downstairs. At the bottom, his legs gave out and he dropped to his knees. His father stood, looking up at Jake, one slippery hand on the bar, and another on the wet spot growing on his shirt. Fear stirred in his watery eyes.

"Jake don't—"

David's hand slid down the bar, tipping over a half-filled bottle of whisky. He fell, hitting the concrete ground facedown. The clinking of the glass stopped, and silence entered.

Jake stumbled over to his father and turned him over; blood spilled from his wounds. "Dad?" David's eyes fluttered. "Stay with me Dad." Jake tore open his father's shirt.

"Jake," David managed.

"You're going to be alright, Dad, just hang in there." Jake pressed on the bloody wells with his own shirt. "Help!" he screamed. "Someone help us!" When no one came, he got up and ran out, yelling for help. In the back of his mind, he sought to catch a glimpse of the assailant.

"Jake, help me, please!"

Jake suppressed his urge to go after the shooter, and he came to his dad's side. "You'll be okay, Dad." Jake's hands were slick with blood.

"I don't want to die." David's voice grew faint. He reached and squeezed Jake's arm with a limpish hand.

"You'll be okay. Dad." *No, please no.* Jake pushed down harder on the soaked shirt.

"Jake, I'm feeling lightheaded . . . if I don't make it, just know that—" Blood was seeping from David's mouth.

"You'll be fine, Dad. You'll make it," Jake comforted.

"Just know that it's not your fault," David said and reached toward Jake with pale fingers. He coughed and a few more drops came out of his parted lips. "Nothing is your fault."

"I know Dad. It's okay, try to keep your strength." Jake kept one hand pressed down on the wounds and used the other to wipe the sweat and blood off of David's forehead. His face was pure agony.

"I should've been a better father, and none of this would have happened." He choked and his eyes fluttered closed.

"It's okay, Dad, everything is okay. Everything will be okay," Jake said, and then wailed, "Help! Someone please!"

David's eyes opened halfway. "I love you, Son," he whispered, and his body convulsed as he took his last breath.

"I love you, Dad, you'll be okay, I promise!" Jake bargained, but David did not respond. Jake checked his father's pulse. Nothing. He checked it again and shook David's body. "Wake up, damn it!" He pounded his chest. Then he hugged his Dad close and blood stained his face. He hugged him closer and cried.

After a moment, Jake got up and kicked over a chair and table in the middle of the room. He jumped and stomped on the table until it splintered off into pieces. Then he ran outside, knowing the killer was already gone. *Fuck! I'll fucking kill you!* He went back into the bar, looked around, grabbed the nearest bottle, sat down, back against the bar, and drank.

~ ~ ~

Hours later, he came to—head throbbing, vision blurred. It took him a minute to recall what had happened before blacking out. *Dad!* He panicked, looking around. Jake was back in his own room. Did I dream this? he wondered, but the liquor taste in his mouth told him otherwise. He tried to get up, but dizziness made him sit. He made himself stand through the haziness and stumbled downstairs, rambling, and found a skinny, sad-eyed hotel manager cleaning up the blood.

"I'm sorry, sir, they took him to the morgue, it's two streets down to the left."

Jake sprinted out. He kicked in the door and saw David. Pale. Bloated. Dead.

Someone was saying something to Jake, but he couldn't hear. He spun around and punched the closest wall.

"Fuck!" Two knuckles started bleeding; the sudden impact revived the pain in his head. A lump formed in his throat, his stomach churned.

"Sir, I'm so sorry," someone babbled. "We'll need you to make a decision today or tomorrow . . . We can't keep him in this heat." The temperature had been unusually high the last couple of days.

Jake's whole body shook.

"You can pick up his belongings on the desk there." He pointed to a paper bag. It was streaked with blood from the mortician's glove.

Jake put his hand on his father's chest and closed his eyes. The tears flowed freely, in a salty bitter stream.

March 2061 – Present Day
Anna Faroe – The Red Rocks
Goldfield, Nevada

Anna made her way to Goldfield after Jake didn't come back for over two weeks. It was hot and wet. The weather, just like her life, was not making sense as of late. Her dress, shawl, and shoes did not withstand the fierceness of the tepid rain.

The hotel where Jake was staying was not hard to find. The rumors spread fast around town of the shooting. The townspeople were scared to go in. As she walked in, she noticed a bullet casing on the ground. She picked it up, a sinking feeling in her stomach.

"Where is he?" Anna demanded.

The hotel owner pointed upstairs.

There were only five rooms, and Anna heard talking from one of them. *It's him.* She let herself in.

He sat on the bed, exhausted, bruised, and worn. His eyes red and puffy, his breath sour. He looked smaller somehow, as if a piece of him was gone.

"Jake!" She ran to him. He grabbed her and kissed her. It was a slow kiss, a kiss of sadness, a kiss craved by comfort.

Jake pulled away and she noticed a tin can sitting on the bed. It was painted a rose gold with a wrap-around label covering the bottom half. White thick letters ran along the curvature.

"Jake, what happened?"

"I um . . ." He looked into her eyes. "I don't know." He put his hand on the tin can.

"Is that—?" She knew the answer.

Jake looked at her, he didn't move or speak.

"Is it your . . ."

He nodded.

"I'm so sorry, Jake." Anna took him in her arms and held him tight.

"I still can't, I just . . ." He began to rock back and forth.

"Shhh. We don't have to talk right now."

Jake buried his head in her chest. "Thank you, thank you, thank you," he repeated, and then he fell asleep in Anna's arms.

March 2061 – Present Day
Anna Faroe – The Red Rocks
Goldfield, Nevada

Anna managed to clean Jake up and put him in bed. He slept for the next forty-eight hours, mumbling in response to restless dreams.

On day three, she woke him up for dinner. "You have to eat something," she said. Jake rolled over and put the blanket over his head. "Jake, we have to start thinking about going home." He threw the covers off, muttered something under his breath, and then got up. They sat in silence for a while. Anna watched as Jake pushed the pieces of steak and potatoes around on his plate, not taking a single bite.

Anna felt an ache in her heart, an ache of empathy. He needed to talk. "Jake, I—"

"They fucking killed him." He threw his bread down, scattering crumbs all over the table and floor.

Anna looked at Jake, shocked, mouth open. She thought it had been an accident.

"Shot twice." Jake got up and started pacing.

"Jake, I'm so sorry. I can't believe this." Anna walked over and tried to touch his arm but he pulled it away.

"I'm sorry, I'm not mad at you. I'm just so angry, so confused." Jake's chest heaved.

"Do they know why or who?" Anna asked.

"No, I couldn't find anything out." Jake leaned against the tiled counter next to the kitchen area to the left of the bed and crossed his arms. "I don't know how I'm supposed to feel, Anna. He was the jerk that abandoned me, and now . . . when I finally, when we finally . . . and now he's gone."

Anna got closer to Jake and took his hands in hers.

"I don't know Anna. I don't know how to feel. Maybe I should have spent more time with him."

"Jake, you can't think like that," she said, but she knew her words were worthless. "Be happy for the time you had with him."

She pulled him in closer, and he trembled in her arms.

"We have to pick up his things," he said, after a moment.

"What are you talking about?"

"His keys. I got them. The keys to his place, I mean. They were with his belongings in the mor—" He choked on the words. After a moment, Jake cleared his throat and said, "The hotel manager told me where he lives. I'd like to go there before we return to Livingsworth."

"Okay," she said. "We will."

~ ~ ~

The next day, they stood in David's small room. It was situated in the back of a brothel, almost as if meant to be a closet. Paint slid off the bare, gray, water-damaged walls. There was a tiny desk and chair, as if meant for a child. A book lay on the desk. The print was old fashioned, as if from a vintage printing press. The title, barely visible, read: *The Metropolitans*. Anna thumbed through it while Jake sat on the bed, staring blankly at the wall, sipping on a bottle of whiskey. The book had titles and prints of his mother's journal, David had made a copy for himself. On the last page, Anna found a lose picture of Jake from when he was younger. He hadn't change much since.

"There's something in the mattress." Jake bounced on the bed, then burrowed into it. He pulled out a cigar box and opened it. Inside, lay a wad of Red Rock notes, and several pieces of jewelry.

March 2061 – Present Day
Bill Vos – The Red Rocks
Kingman, Nevada

Bill felt sick to his stomach as he waited for Tommy to let him into his office. Muffled moans escaped the closed door. He took out Emmy's ring and closed his hand over it. *I thought I'd feel better, Emmy. When I gave up the search for this man, your murderer, years ago, I thought I was done, but I wasn't. And now, I feel just as empty as I did when I knew he was alive. I wish you were here, to guide me. How do I know if what I did was right? I'm so lost without you.*

Bill slid his fingers up and down the hilt of his gun. Tommy might try something to get rid of the last witness—me, Bill thought. I hope he does, so I never have to see his face again. Bill shook with anger. Shooting the man responsible for Emmy's death did not bring him the peace he wanted, and now, this pathetic sloth of man knew what he was capable of first-hand. Hatred stewed within him.

Ten minutes later, the door to the office opened. Tommy stood inside in a silk robe, gray chest hairs peeking out. "Hey Bill, come on in."

Bill walked through the door, finding a half-naked, thick, busty blonde gathering her clothes. As soon as she left, he said, "It's done."

"Well, well." Tommy pushed his glasses up toward his pointed nose. "Happy to hear that. Did it go as planned? No witnesses?"

"Yes," Bill said.

"Great!" Tommy clapped. "To be frank with you, I already knew."

Bill's dark eyes clouded over.

"I had a member of my crew settle in Goldfield for a while to tell me when the deed was done. In any case, glad it all worked out," Tommy said, amusement in his eye.

"Are there any news of my mother-in-law?"

"She's still in the hospital," Tommy said nonchalantly.

Bill's fingers itched to grab the gun and pull the trigger. He didn't say anything.

"Here are the hospital papers," Tommy finally said, understanding what Bill wanted.

Bill looked the papers over. The prognosis wasn't optimistic. He filed them away into his leather satchel.

"You ready for more deliveries then?"

It's good to stay busy, and Tommy was his only way of getting Emmy's mother the care she needed. I can give her a few more comfortable months, Bill thought. Emmy would want that.

"Yes."

Tommy opened his drawer and took out four packages. "This one's batteries, this one's cigarettes, and these two are very special *herbal* spices, if you know what I mean." Tommy grinned.

Bill didn't smile back.

"Here are your four clients," Tommy continued and slid over the delivery schedule.

"Deadline for delivery?"

"As soon as possible."

"Okay then. I will report back." Bill stood up and collected the packages.

"Do you maybe want to rest for a day here? I'll set you up: get you a bath, a massage, a girl—anything you want."

Bill put his wide-brim hat on and walked out the door.

March 2061 – Present Day
Jake Deen – The Red Rocks
Livingsworth, Nevada

Jake lay in Anna's room, staring at the ceiling, watching the birds fly on the walls, each one surrounded by a small halo. He leaned over and grabbed the vile of volt from the nightstand, put two drops into his eye, and downed his glass of whiskey. He felt good. He felt very good. But he knew what could make him feel even better.

He rubbed the stubble on his chin. "Anna?" No answer. "Anna, get over here!" he yelled. He heard footsteps, then the door opened slowly.

"What Jake?" Anna stood, arms crossed over her chest, eyeing the liquid in the vile. "You shouldn't be doing that."

Jake followed her gaze. "What are you, the volt police?" He laughed, then stood up and stumbled toward her. "Get over here! I want to fu—"

"Are you serious?" She looked at him in disgust. "What are you doing, Jake? You have to stop this nonsense. For a week all you've been doing is getting fucked up in this room."

"Not true," Jake giggled, and tried to take off his boxers. "I also do you."

Anna rolled her eyes.

"Come on, come over here and fuck me!"

"Don't talk to me like that."

"But isn't that your job?"

"What did you say?" Anna squinted her eyes.

"You know, to fuck people?"

Anna turned around and slammed the door.

"Whore!" Jake yelled after her. Then he put his fingers over his eyes and his mouth opened in a silent scream. He held onto the wall as he walked to the door.

"Anna? Anna, I'm sorry." He stepped out. "Anna?" He looked around, but she was gone. "Fuck! What the fuck?" Jake fell to his knees put his head in his hands. "I'm sorry, Anna. If you can hear me, I'm sorry," he said, louder this time. Then he stumbled back into the bedroom, squeezed the rest of the vile in his eye, took the whiskey, and headed for the bathroom.

March 2061 – Present Day
Jake Deen – The Red Rocks
Livingsworth, Nevada

Drip. The first bottle of whiskey had broken in his angry hand, and now, blood was sliding out of his vein onto the floor, forming a warm puddle. It felt good.

Drip. He made a new cut on his forearm, using a piece of jagged glass.

Drip. Drip. He fucking hated himself. Hated himself for being weak. Hated himself for hurting Anna. Hated himself for not being able to save his dad. Why hadn't he been there? If he came out of his room five minutes earlier, his dad might still be alive.

Slurp. The whiskey ran down his chin. He could've had a fresh start, and now he was nothing again—a piece of shit, a failure, just trash on earth bringing trouble to the people he loved. *I . . . I wasn't meant to be.*

Drip. Drip. Drip. Slurp. The bottle fell down with a clank, and rolled away nearly empty. *Who would have done this? Who could've killed Dad?* Jake's head was dull, but he could not stop replaying the devastating scene in his head. Shots. Dad. Morgue. Dead.

Drip. Drip Drip. Jake turned over the woven hamper next to him and took out a piece of clothing. He put it over his wet arm.

Clink. Something rolled out on the floor. He picked it up—a bullet casing. He flipped it in his hand; it had a cross etched in the flattened back. He lifted the piece of clothing—Anna's dress. *Why would she have this?*

Another memory wiggled its way into his mind. He searched his pockets and took out the casing he had saved from when Bill had taught him how to shoot. He looked at both side by side.

"Aaaaaaah!" He threw the casings against the wall. Red blood gushed from his arm. Then everything went black.

March 2061 – Present Day
Anna Faroe – The Red Rocks
Livingsworth, Nevada

Anna knocked on the bathroom door. "What are you doing in there?"

There was no response.

"Jake? Open the door." Anna knocked harder. She waited, no response. "You open up this goddamn door right now!" She heard a shuffle, but still no response.

Bam! She hit the door with her shoulder, but it didn't open. She kicked it. *Bam!* The door flew open and slammed against the wall. She looked around. "Jake!" she shrieked.

Jake slid down the wall he was sitting against, and a shard of glass dropped from his hands. His eyelids fluttered.

"Damn it, Jake," she said through tears as she wrapped his arm. He was pale and quiet. Anger overwhelmed her.

"What were you thinking?" she cried, and leaned him back against the wall, then ran to her medicine cabinet.

A sob escaped her as she tried to concentrate: peroxide, gauze, gloves, thread, needle. *I can do this, I can do this.*

"Jake?" She shook him lightly. "Jake, can you hear me?" No response. She bit her lip and leaned over, accidently pressing his vein; a thick stream of blood oozed onto her fingers. "Goddamn it!" She turned away and spat, bile rising in her throat.

Anna managed to stitch Jake up, and clean him up. She checked his pulse, then dragged him to the room, and put him on the bed.

She laughed to herself, then went to the kitchen. "What am I supposed to do now?" She unlocked her liquor cabinet and retrieved a bottle of homemade lingonberry vodka—a Swedish ex-client brought her a bottle each time he visited. She took two shots, then pulled out a cigarette pack, lit one up, took a drag, and closed her eyes, lightheaded. She realized for the first time that her body was drenched in sweat.

She checked on Jake one more time. A light pink color had crept back into his complexion, and he was snoring.

Anna sighed and pursed her lips, shaking her head back and forth.

She got gloves and went into the bathroom. A metallic smell hung in the air, a smell of lurking death. She brought her arm to her forehead and leaned against the nearest wall. She took several deep breaths before starting to clean. After a half an hour, when she finally finished wiping the blood and liquor off the floor, she got herself another drink, and sat down on the couch.

I love you, but this has got to stop.

March 2061 – Present Day
Jake Deen – The Red Rocks
Livingsworth, Nevada

Jake opened one eye, head pounding, arms screaming. Weakness spread through his body, one muscle at a time—each movement an agonizing battle. Outside, a woodpecker worked hard for its meal, each peck drilling a nail through his brain.

The memory of the night before trickled in piece by piece: the slicing of veins, Anna's horrified voice, distant pain. He surveyed the room and saw Anna sleeping on a chair across from the bed.

"You're awake." She opened her eyes; they were red from crying. The sight tore Jake's heart apart.

"I'm . . . I'm sorry, I don't know what I was thinking," he said.

Anna stared at him, not saying a word. She looked spent.

"I don't know what else to say, I was just stupid."

"Yes, yes you were."

"What can I do to make this better?" he asked, sighing as he sat up.

"Jake, I've been in abusive relationships before. Getting aggressive with me—I won't stand for it." She stood up and opened the only window in the room, letting the outside air filter in.

"I know, I'm an asshole. A fucking selfish asshole. I'll do anything, I'll stop drinking. Anything you want."

"Yes, you will. And what you did in the bathroom . . ." Anna trailed off.

"That was a mistake. I don't know what I was thinking. I was high and it felt good because . . . well . . . because it didn't feel like anything."

"You scared me," Anna said.

"Anna, I love you. I don't ever want to do anything to hurt you. I promise you, it will never happen again."

"If it does, it will be the last time we see each other," Anna said, and walked out of the room.

First, I'll stop drinking, he thought. Make things right with Anna. Then, I'll find Bill. I'll find him, and I'll kill him.

April 2061 – Present Day
Anna Faroe – The Red Rocks
Livingsworth, Nevada

"That's it! I can't handle this anymore!" Anna yelled. Jake had relapsed yet again. He had been on and off, and on and off, for a month. She had poured out all of the alcohol in the house, but Jake kept sneaking out to get more while she slept. He was delusional, talking about avenging his father when he could barely stand. She was on her last straw.

"I'm grieving!" Jake's eyes were empty.

"You're not! All you're doing is killing yourself. You have to stop!"

"And who are you to tell me anything?" Jake screamed.

Anna stood, blood boiling. "I gave up my life for you. I gave up my job."

"Spreading your legs for other people isn't something to be proud of. I saved you from that job."

"You think you saved me?!"

Jake's eyebrows creased with confusion. "I . . . well . . . yeah I saved you!"

Anna took out a bag and began packing her clothes.

"What are you doing? You're leaving me now?"

"You think about what you are doing here. You don't want to quit. You don't want to get better. You don't want me to help you. I told you, you will lose me if you keep going this way."

"Fine!" Jake howled. "I don't need you."

Anna zipped up her bag and made her way toward the door.

"Who are you going to see, Sebastián? Adrian? Who?!"

"I can't keep having this conversation," Anna said. Jake's drinking was making him paranoid. He thought she was seeing her clients again, secretly meeting with them at night while he was sleeping.

"Who is it?!"

"I can't do this anymore, Jake. Goodbye." But as she opened the door to leave, she realized she could not.

That night, Jake begged all night for her forgiveness.

May 2061 – Present Day
Anna Faroe – The Red Rocks
Livingsworth, Nevada

One month later, Anna slid into bed next to Jake. "Come eat," she whispered in his ear, lingering to give him a nibble.

He opened his eyes and smiled. He flipped her underneath him and kissed her neck.

"The food will get cold, you know," she said.

"I don't care," he said, and went beneath the blankets, moving down to her stomach, then to her hips, then lower, leaving a trail of wet kisses. Anna sighed and Jake brought his face up to hers.

Moments after, they lay in each other's arms, basking in the afterglow before rising to eat. It felt like it did when they just met—perfect, easy.

"So," Jake began. "I was thinking it's time for me to go back to Bobby's and work." Jake scooped up a spoonful of porridge. "I'm down to the last of the money I found at my father's place, so one of us has to find work. I want to support you, Anna. Just like I promised I would." Anna knew he was right. They didn't have much left. She also knew he would never let her take on a few clients, even the ones she wasn't physical with. At this moment, she didn't want to either.

Anna looked into his eyes. "Are you sure you're ready? You've been sober for a nearly a month, and I don't want anything to change that. People will ask, and you'll have to talk about your father . . ."

"I'll be okay," Jake said, his emerald eyes clear.

"Promise me you won't do anything stupid?"

"Like volt or drinking? No, I told you, I'm done with that."

"No, like try to look for your father's killer." She looked at him, sternly. She knew he suspected who the murderer was, but didn't tell her.

"I won't, I promise. I'll just go to Bobby's to see if he has work for me. That's all."

"Okay," Anna nodded. "I trust you."

May 2061 – Present Day
Jake Deen – The Red Rocks
Livingsworth, Nevada

Jake put on a black T-shirt, a fresh pair of jeans, his old ad-checkered sweater, and a pair of faded work boots. He brushed out his blond hair, now falling down past his shoulders. He would find out what he needed to, one way or another. Jake stared into the mirror, his eyes shining bright. He was rested, he was clean. He shaved his growing beard, one lump of hair after another falling into the basin. He had to find him. He'd fucking kill him.

Jake walked into Bobby's, and his jaw dropped when he saw Bobby waving a sword at the marshal. A gun lay on the floor a few feet away from the marshal's feet.

"No one has to get hurt," the badge-wearing dirtbag said carefully.

"You're right, no one does." Bobby walked closer to the stocky man. The bar was empty but for the three of them. It smelled of ale.

"Give me the cassette tape, Bobby, and I will leave you alone. I promise."

"How stupid do you think I am?" He began to circle the marshal. "Do you know how much money you took from me? Can you even count?" Bobby roared. "I work my ass off for this fucking bar, and you think you can come in and fuck with my business?"

"Bobby, calm yourself," the marshal said.

Jake stood in the back, watching the drama unfold, but kept his knife handy.

"Fuck you! I will turn you in and you will go to jail forever. Everything I need is on this tape."

"Give me the tape!" the marshal screeched, and leaped toward Bobby, who sidestepped and kicked the marshal in the ass.

"You piece of shit, you dumbfuck! You'll never make money here. If it's not me, it's someone else." The marshal flailed his arms, his face perspiring profusely.

"Oh no?" Bobby said, a mean twinkle in his eye. "I have you on tape now, and I will turn you in if you don't stop taking my money!"

"I take what's mine," the marshal said. "You don't think I know what goes on in your back room? You don't think I know what deliveries you facilitate? I can get an order for the real police to come and shut you down."

"Then why don't you? I'll give them the tape of you taking that money as a bribe. Who do you think they'll care about more, a government official or a small-time bar owner?"

"Don't you dare!" The marshal marched over to Bobby, but Bobby kicked him in the chest. When he stumbled, Bobby pushed him to the ground and stepped on his arm. Then he brought the sword down precisely to cut off a small part of the marshal's left index finger.

"Aaaaaaah!" The marshal screamed and Bobby lifted his foot off the arm. The marshal got up and ran toward the door, holding his finger. "You freaking maniac!"

"Don't ever come back here," Bobby called after him.

Jake stood in the corner, his mouth open. Maybe he *could* get Bobby to help with Bill. Then he thought about it some more. This was his own battle.

"Oh, Jake. Hey," Bobby said, as he wiped down his sword. "How long were you standing there?"

"Long enough, Bobby. Nice moves."

Bobby grinned. "Sometimes you have to fight for what's right."

Yes, Jake thought. Yes you do. He went to give Bobby a one-armed hug and pat on the back.

"So what are your plans now? You staying or you going?"

"If you'll have me, I'd like to come back to work," said Jake.

"If it was anyone else, Jake, I wouldn't but you"—Bobby pointed at Jake—"but you I'll take back in."

"I'm that good, huh?" Jake joked.

Bobby laughed. "Don't flatter yourself. I just need someone to play chess with during downtime." He walked to the bar and poured himself a drink. "Oh, I wanted to let you know . . . Bill stopped by last month. I told him I hadn't seen you."

"Oh yeah?" A sudden rage came over Jake.

"He also stopped by again two days ago and said he'd be back tomorrow." Bobby poured Jake a club soda, who drank it thirstily, plans evolving in his tempered mind.

"Thanks for the message. I guess I'll see him tomorrow."

May 2061 – Present Day
Jake Deen – The Red Rocks
Livingsworth, Nevada

Jake felt the gun in his back pocket. He spat and shook his head, then sped up his walk. The day was overcast and windless. The air was full of moisture and it left a thin film on his skin. He lit a cigarette to calm his nerves.

I promise you, Anna, after this is all over, I will do right by you. I will marry you and give you the best life in the world, and I promise to live every day to make you the happiest woman on this earth.

"Hey, ready to work?" Bobby asked as soon as Jake came through the door.

"Yes." Jake smiled.

"Glad to see you are back into your stride after just one day. Oh yeah, Bill's in the back."

"Oh," Jake responded, face solemn, thoughts racing. He coughed. "I'll be right back."

"I'll be here," Bobby said.

Jake walked into the back room. Bill sat, tired dark eyes covered by the shadow of his hat. His jean jacket was wrinkled and his hair lose. He didn't look like his normal well put together self.

"Jake, good to see you. It's been a long time. I thought you moved and that we might not see each other again. It would be a shame not to ride with you anymore."

"I was busy, needed to run some errands," Jake said coldly.

Bill nodded. "I needed to run a few errands myself."

I'm sure you did, Jake thought to himself. "Do you mind if we go outside?" he asked.

Bill's eyebrows lifted slightly. "Why?"

"I'd rather not be in a bar," Jake lied.

"Don't you put in hours here when we're not out riding?" Bill questioned.

"Not for the last few months," Jake said.

"I see." Bill gave a nod, understanding in his eyes. "Okay. Let's go out back." Bill stood up and made his way to the door; Jake noted the pistols hanging on his belt. He always knew they were there, but today, they were more threatening.

The area behind the bar was fenced off, the only way out was through the stables to the right. The smell of horses' manure was overpowering, and the hard ground was thick with dust. In the background, spotted green mountains were housing an early morning fog.

"I need to ask you something," Jake said, and moved his head side to side until his neck cracked.

Bill's expression turned serious. "What is it you need to know?"

"What were these extra errands you needed to run?"

Bill furrowed his brow. "Why do you want to know?"

"Were they the same type of errands that you used to run in Metropolitans, after Emmy's death?"

"And if they were?" Bill's hand moved closer to his belt.

"Were they errands for a man in Goldfield?" Jake spat, then took out a bullet casing from his pocket, and threw it at Bill, who caught it swiftly.

Bill looked the casing over. "Did you know the man?" Bill's tone deepened and hatred flashed in his eyes.

"He was my father."

"He was your father?" Bill exclaimed, but there was no sincerity in his voice.

"It *was* you then," Jake growled. "Yes, he was my father!"

Bill's face clouded over. "Jake, I didn't know he was your father. I'm sorry."

"You fucking killed my father!" Jake tried to keep his voice down, but the words came out in a loud yelp.

"It wasn't personal," Bill said carefully.

"It wasn't personal?" Jake spat. "It was personal to me?!"

"I didn't know that you two were family. I would've never accepted the job if I knew. You are my friend."

"Sure you didn't know." Jake took out his gun and started waving it around. "We're not talking about a delivery gone bad here, you killed someone! You killed an innocent old man!" Jake noticed Bill eyeing his gun bearing hand.

"Jake, I didn't know. I would not have taken the job if I knew. You know the man I am."

"I don't know you at all! Not anymore, or maybe I never did!"

"You do, Jake. You know. You are my friend and I don't want to hurt you. I didn't realized you two were family. I didn't think about it before." Bill looked at Jake intently.

"Now I see the resemblance," he said almost to where Jake couldn't hear.

"I started thinking of you as a close friend. I invited you over to have dinner!" Jake shouted. "Is that why you declined? Because you planned to kill my father?"

"I didn't know he was your father. How would I? You said you and your father didn't see each other for years!" Defense bolted in Bill's voice.

"We didn't,"—Jake paused—"And you know, I saw you as a mentor, as a father figure even," Jake's voice quieted and became loud again. "I can't even think, who the fuck are you? You're the same as you were all those years ago. Killing innocent men for pay!"

"He was not innocent," Bill stated. Jake could sense his irritation.

"Tell me then! I want to know what he did to deserve this!"

"You know I can't do that. I'm not getting you involved."

"You're a fucking coward." Jake shook his head.

"I understand your anger. Perhaps it's best if we go inside before someone gets hurt."

Jake pointed his gun toward Bill's head. They stood in alert silence. Then, Jake said, "You gotta give me something man; it's the least you can do. I need to know why he was targeted." Jake was shaking. "I'm asking you man to man."

Bill looked at Jake for a long time. "I can't Jake. I can only tell you that he was not a good man."

"What did he do that was so awful? To deserve such a cold, painful death?"

"He was not a good man, Jake. You don't want to risk your life for him"—Bill paused—"You don't know him."

"And you do?" Jake yelled.

"I know about his past, even before he moved to the Red Rocks."

"So, what?" Jake stomped. "Tell me!"

Bill looked from side to side and said, "He was involved in my wife's death."

"What? Who told you that? Your gangster boss?" Jake screamed. "I don't believe that for a second! He's a liar!"

"It's the truth, Jake. I have the police report from Emily's attack. Your father's photograph is the photograph of the man who went to jail for her murder."

"Fuck you!" Jake waved the gun and his other hand touched the back of his head, a throb pecking its way through.

"I can ride out and get his release form from my house right now. Just put your gun down."

"I don't think so," Jake said. "You're lying to me."

"Now, think about this, you don't want to do this."

"Oh yes I do." Jake cocked his gun.

Bill put his hand on his own pistol. "He's a murderer, Jake."

"Fuck you, you don't know shit!" said Jake, voice near hysteria.

"What purpose do I have to lie to you? You're pointing your gun at me."

"That's exactly why. You'll tell me anything to get me to back off."

"You forget that I, too, have a gun." Bill brought the weapon in front of him. "Why don't we end this now? You go back inside, and I'll be on my way."

"I don't think so," Jake said, ready to shoot.

"Fine," Bill replied. Before Jake could fire, Bill seized Jake's gun with his free hand and tossed it aside.

"Fuck!" Jake roared.

Bill holstered his own gun. "Does that mean we're done here?"

"Why don't you fight me like a man?" Jake took out his knife.

"Jake, I don't want to do this."

"What, you nervous? You should be, you bastard!" Jake leaped at him with the knife, and Bill avoided his lunge. Bill got his own knife out.

"Seems stupid not to use your gun," Jake commented.

"I fight fair."

"Nothing fair about killing an unarmed man from afar."

"And killing an unarmed woman on the streets is fair?" Bill's nostril's flared.

"My father was a drunk! He could never kill anyone!"

"I have no reason to lie to you."

"Your whole life is a lie! You sick fuck!" Jake dove at Bill and sliced Bill across the chest; a trickle of blood made its way down his clean shirt. Bill winced and kicked Jake it the knee, Jake took a few steps back, almost losing his balance.

They circled each other, waiting for the opportunity to strike.

"You don't want to do this Jake," Bill repeated. Jake could hear the certainty in Bill's tone.

"I'm winning, so I think I *do* want to do this."

"I warned you." Bill spun around, slicing Jake's knife-bearing hand.

Jake grunted and stepped backward, and then charged into Bill, tackling him to the ground and landing on top of him. "You son of a bitch!" They rolled around until Jake got the upper hand and straddled Bill. He punched Bill in the ear. Bill shook his head, disoriented, several drops of blood dripping out. Jake continued to punch Bill's ribs and stomach. "I got you, you motherfucker!" Jake yelled, but at that moment, Bill caught his arm and pressed his hand into Jake's throat. Jake weaved out of Bill's hold. Bill kicked his legs up trying to knee Jake in the back, but Jake didn't budge and started punching Bill in his face. Bill hit Jake twice near his diaphragm. Jake gasped for air, but kept hitting Bill's bloody nose and cheeks. A third punch to the delicate area made Jake jerk to the left. He didn't notice Bill's hand was still holding the knife—

Pain erupted through him as the cold, sharp steel entered his side. His vision blurred, and his strength gave. He coughed and fell on top of Bill, who slowly rolled out from underneath him.

"Jake." He flipped Jake over on his back. "Can you hear me?"

Jake couldn't move, the pain overcame his ability to speak. Bill looked into his eyes. Jake grabbed the knife.

"Jake don't!" Bill pleaded.

Jake took the knife out of his side and watched the blood pour out of his fresh wound.

"You son of a bitch," Jake managed, the agony enveloping his words. He tried to get up, but couldn't.

Bill stood up, but then leaned back down next to Jake to examine the cut. Jake stared at Bill, alarmed. He didn't say anything—he couldn't—but his expression cried out for help. Bill took off his shirt, put it in Jake's hands and pressed it to the wound. "Hold this here," he said. "You'll need to get help or you will bleed out."

Jake choked as he tried to breathe.

"You'll make it through this." Bill took out his gun and fired two shots in the air. "Someone will be here soon to help you," he said. "Goodbye, Jake. I hope we never see each other again."

With that, Jake watched Bill stagger to his horse. He stared at the sky, losing life with every second.

May 2061 – Present Day
Anna Faroe – The Red Rocks
Livingsworth, Nevada

Anna clutched the girl in front of her as their horse galloped at a phenomenal speed, each turn a near fall.

A blond curly-haired girl had turned up at her house and told her they'd found Jake after hearing gun shots outside of Bobby's bar. Jake was wounded, falling in and out of consciousness. Even before the girl had arrived, Anna had felt sick to her stomach, already knowing that something bad had happened.

Shock, disbelief, and hope cycled through her heart.

When they arrived at Bobby's, Anna ran outside, through the back of the bar, to find a group of people gathered around a motionless figure on the ground.

"Nooooooooooooo!" A high-pitched cry escaped her lips. The knot in her gut tightened. She knelt down next to Jake and brushed the hair off of his face.

A man with bloody hands and medical supplies sat next to Jake, his eyes deep pools of sympathy. "I'm sorry, we did everything we could, but I'm afraid it's too late," the man said. "He only has a few minutes left."

"No," she sobbed. "Please Jake, stay with me. Please," she cried. "I love you," she said through the tears, holding Jake in her arms, rocking back and forth.

He opened his eyes; it took him several seconds to focus. "I love you too, Anna."

"You are so good. We are so good." A sob escaped her lips. "I need you here with me. We can start a family and live together. Please, God, I'll do anything!"

Jake's breath got shallower; fresh blood stained his lips.

"No, please no," Anna whimpered.

"I love—" Jake's eyes closed.

"Open your eyes, Jake, open your eyes!" she screamed, but nothing happened. "Somebody do something!"

The crowd was quiet.

"Why, why?" she cried and touched his hair and kissed his face. She held him for hours, holding his lifeless form in her arms.

Bobby and his workers came and went, checking on her. A few sat by her side. She sat there until the sun set, soaked in sweat, tears, and Jake's blood.

"We have to take him ma'am, I'm sorry." The town mortician stood behind Anna looking down.

"No, not yet," Anna whispered. "At least let me say my final goodbye."

The man nodded.

Anna looked into Jake's dead eyes, then squeezed hers shut and rocked back and forth. The tears that she thought had dried up, once again ran down her cheeks. She kissed Jake on the lips and forehead. Then, with a trembling hand, she closed his eyelids. No energy, no more hope. Pain turned to numbness.

"Please, Miss Anna. It's time."

Anna stared as the people took Jake's body away. She held onto his sweater.

"Anna, please come inside." Bobby reached out his hand to her.

She turned and looked at him. "How did this happen?"

"I don't know," he said. "Come on." Bobby helped her up. "Let's get you something to drink."

Anna nodded, dazed, lost. "I need you to tell me," she said in a low voice.

"I will. I'll tell you everything I know."

May 2061 – Present Day
Bill Vos – The Red Rocks
Wells, Nevada

Bill took a swig of moonshine, sat down on his bed, and put his head in his hands. *What have I done? A dear friend gone and all for nothing!*

After his confrontation with Jake, Bill had ridden back to Tommy's who told him that his mother-in-law had passed away. The paperwork from the hospital stated that the pneumonia got worse and her heart stopped. For all Bill knew, Tommy had killed her himself.

He took out Emmy's ring and held it in his palm, then closed his hand. *I don't know what to do now. I've failed you. I've failed myself. If I'd only declined Tommy's favor, Jake would still be alive. Your mother, she might still be alive. Jake's father, no matter how awful, would still be alive.*

He had tried to do the right thing, but now it was all a mess. He took another swallow and remembered what he was taught about post-traumatic stress: calm environment, stable schedule, exercise, food, sleep.

He looked around his room, it looked small. Except for his books, there was nothing that told the story of the man living here. He took out his metal box and grabbed his passports and cash. His eyes fell on the silencer; he picked it up, then put it back in the box.

He needed to disappear.

June 2061 – Present Day
Anna Faroe – The Red Rocks
Livingsworth, Nevada

One month later, Anna paced back and forth in front of Bobby's desk his office. "There is no word from the marshal?"

Bobby shook his head. He was sitting in his leather chair, and he looked tired. His clothes were wrinkled and his facial hair uneven. "It's taking the new Livingsworth marshal some time to get settled after the old one resigned."

"They're so useless! What about your men?" Anna looked thinner than normal and disheveled, her hair messy, her dress grimy.

"The men I sent out said that they didn't find anything useful. Bill had already covered his tracks."

"What about his boss? Did they find his boss? Tommy was it?" Anna's worry lines deepened and a chill ran through her body.

Bobby nodded. "He was the one who told them the town Bill lived in, but when my men got there, Bill's place was abandoned."

"Who are these men? Are they experienced? Are they bounty hunters?" Anna's frustration overtook her tone.

"Yes, one of the men is a bounty hunter," Bobby said. He squished a tiny spider running across the lacquered surface.

"Will he keep looking?"

"Yes, until he finds a better offer."

"I will give him the best offer! What does he want?" She slammed her palm on his desk.

"It's not always about the money. Bill's not going to be easy to find."

"But you said his boss told your men about Bill's place!"

"Yes, but how do we know Bill didn't make a deal with Tommy to send us the wrong way?"

Anna threw her head back and sighed. "There has to be another way."

"I think the only option now is too wait." Bobby ran his hands through his hair, which seemed to carry more gray than before.

"Give me Tommy's address, I'll go there myself," she said. She leaned over the table and looked him in the eyes.

"No, he's a criminal. I won't let you go there."

Anna backhanded a stack of pens off of Bobby's desk. "Give it to me!!!" she demanded.

"No, Anna, I can't let you do this," Bobby said, somber.

"Why not?" Anna's eyes oozed hatred. The office seemed to grow smaller and her blood pounded harder each time he told her he wouldn't do it.

"This man is dangerous. You don't know whose side he's on."

Anna's whole body vibrated with anger. "I don't care what we have to do. Bill has to pay!"

"I'll do everything I can," said Bobby. He got up and took out a bottle of whiskey and two tumblers from his desk drawer. He poured a shot in each and nudged one glass toward her. Anna downed it in one swallow.

August 2061 – Present Day
Anna Faroe – The Red Rocks
Wells, Nevada

Books went flying as Anna hit a baseball bat against the wooden shelf. She struck it one more time and it cracked, more books rained down. "You motherfucker! I hate you!" she yelled. It was almost three months since Jake's death. She was disheveled, in a filthy shirt and ripped pants. One of Bobby's men had told her where Bill's place was, and she'd ridden as fast as she could from Livingsworth to Wells.

Bam! The bookshelf splintered and a piece stuck in Anna's hand. She sat down in the rubble. She knew there had to be a clue, something they'd missed. The walls seemed to laugh at her, holding all the answers, but not letting them go. She hung her head.

"Anna!" Bobby stumbled through the door. "Are you alright?" He motioned to her hand; it was dripping with blood.

"What are you doing here?" She wiped her forehead, leaving a red smear.

"I heard you were riding up by yourself, so I followed you."

"Why?" She shrugged. Their efforts proved fruitless. She felt defeated.

"Jake was a friend. And you are important to him." He sat down next to her. They sat in silence, staring at the cracked wall.

"What am I supposed to do?" Anna finally said.

"The best you can do is go live your life. It's what Jake would've wanted. He'd want you to be happy," Bobby said.

September 2061 – Present Day
Anna Faroe – The Red Rocks
Livingsworth, Nevada

Anna was at her house, packing her living room. She looked at the hummingbird blanket, then at her bursting suitcase and sighed. Her eyes landed on the couch, the first place they were intimate, and she began to tremble. Each part of this house was a memory, a painful one.

With no word from the bounty hunter for months, she had decided it was time to make peace with the fact that she might not get her revenge. She had hoped that burying Jake's ashes would give her an ounce of closure, but it hadn't. She hoped that she had done the right thing by burying him next to his father.

She needed to go far away and start fresh. She sold and donated most of her possessions. She couldn't bring herself to sort through Jake's, so she asked Bobby to hold onto them. She made Bobby promise to tell her if Bill was found. He assured her that he would send her any news that came his way.

The last thing she packed was her notebook, full of memories and thoughts. She looked around, picked up a photo of Jake—the one she found at his father's—and taped it onto a blank page. *You'll always have a piece of my heart, Jake, and I will always carry a small piece of you with me.*

And so she left.

Elizabeth Povarova-Simpson

PART II

May 2062 – Present Day
Anna Faroe – The Red Rocks
Brentwood, Arizona

Anna stood outside the only bookshop in Brentwood, formerly Prescott Valley, drinking a cup of coffee and watching people walk by. A girl skipped along while holding her father's hand, a couple kissed in the dusty street, a woman rode her bicycle. The street was busy, but it was the only busy street in Brentwood—Main Street. The rest were residential, calm, quiet. The town stretched for miles and miles, adobe homes sparsely dotting the parched outskirts. There was an old amusement park, and sometimes she'd see the baskets moving when kids climbed onto the Ferris wheel.

With summer around the corner, she was told to enjoy her days because once the heat fully crept in, she'd be spending most of her time in any shade she could find. It would be her first summer here, after she'd moved nine months ago in September.

"Hey Anna!" A young, medium-height man with olive skin and almond-shaped eyes stepped out of the little brick building behind her. "Come in for a second."

Anna followed the man into the bookstore, into the welcoming smell of old paper and ink.

"What is it, Samien?" she asked her client as he pulled her to the new stack of donated books. This town seemed to attract more and more convalescents. They made good, but fickle clients.

"Look, it's my great-great-grandmother's book." He picked up a copy from the stand. "Take it." He smiled wide and she could hear the excitement in his voice. He was so young.

Anna read the synopsis of a book from 2005, describing a love story of a vampire and werewolf. She was glad that fad didn't continue.

"I never got to meet her, but apparently she became really rich and—" He stopped mid-sentence and ran off to look at something else which caught his eye.

His attention span was getting worse and worse each month. Anna remembered the last client she had had who was in his early twenties. He couldn't keep a conversation going for longer than two minutes—she had timed him. Samien was suffering the same fate as many others in the Metropolitans; the ads were taking a toll on his mind. His parents had sent him to the Red Rocks, telling him to take as long as he needed. His ability to concentrate was improving, but his sense of reality was fragile. Every week during their trips to the book store, he announced yet another famous author as being his distant relative. Anna knew she could help.

The white-haired bookstore owner peered disapprovingly over her glasses as Samien darted from one aisle to the next. "Look over here, an old comic book! Wow! You cannot find these at all anymore in the Red Rocks. Not ones you can touch anyway."

She walked over to look at the comic books, the covers of which were wrinkled and scratched, except for the few in mint condition protected by plastic sleeves.

"It's neat," she said, watching him flip through a comic book about a man dressed up as a bat.

She walked to the new arrivals section; her chest tightened when saw a man with green eyes staring back at her from a magazine cover—guilt nagged at her. It's been a year since Jake died, but she still felt his presence. She knew he wouldn't approve of her taking on clients.

"We have to go!" Samien was shaking and his eyes held panic; he ran out of the store.

"What is it?" Anna asked him outside.

"It's happening again, Anna, take me to your home, please, I can't." Samien squeezed her hand.

"Okay, come with me, everything will be okay."

"I can't, I can't." Samien started wailing as he walked, his gulps for air were short and shallow. A group of teenagers pointed and whispered toward their direction.

"We'll be there soon."

"I can't see anything!" he shouted; a kit of pigeons picking at stale bits of bread bolted from the sudden noise.

"My hands, my body, they're numb! I can't feel anything!"

Anna put his arm over her shoulder and helped him to her new home—a small bungalow at the edge of town. Her thoughts wandered back to Jake. His wild hair and calloused hands. His touch. Then thoughts sped up to the conversation she had with him before he went to Bobby's—she knew he was going to do something impulsive—she felt it. She should've stopped him. I can't think like this, she told herself and brought her focus back to Samien.

When they got to her place, half an hour later, Samien asked. "Am I sick to the point of no return? Do I have admania?" He lay on her couch, his dark hair wet. He looked sad and confused.

"No." Anna wiped his dripping forehead with a warm cloth, he was shivering. "You had an attack, but it's subsiding. Tell me, what did it feel like?"

"I don't know. I just felt like I couldn't breathe, I couldn't walk or speak, and my mind flashed neon, it flashed with ads, ads I've seen a lot in the Metropolitans. Some ads I've never seen before. At least I don't think I have?"

"You'll be okay. This is a side effect of your brain becoming overwhelmed, but it's not admania." He had left the Metropolitans just in time, she thought. "Something must have triggered it at the store, can you think of anything?"

"I don't know. I just felt like I was *in* the ads, playing a role, but I couldn't get out."

"Where were you?"

"In the middle of the neon New York City streets. It was like being in a mall on Black Friday. Billboards, trademarks, logos, spokespeople—all competing for a millisecond of my attention. I even recalled the fabricated smells. Did you know they are sold to the highest bidder? It's so they can interact with the irrational part of your brain that will make you take out your wallet." Samien twitched and his eyes rolled into the back of his head. His body jerked.

"Shh. Shh." Anna dripped a tiny drop of volt, the low dosage kind you got from a doctor, into a glass of water and made him drink it. His eyes pinpointed, then dilated, and his breath slowed. She brought him a cup of chamomile tea and put her hummingbird blanket over him. "Get some rest." This one will take a lot of work to recover, she thought.

A knock came on the door. Anna opened it to find a hooded man in front of her. He handed her a letter. It was one of Bobby's couriers.

"Ma'am."

"Thank you," Anna said and watched the courier ride off before she opened it up. The letter read:

> I hope you're doing well. The bounty hunters brought back word that they had a nibble on a lead, but the trail went cold before they could pursue it. I wish I had better news. I want to find

him as much as you do. I will write again next month.

Anna grabbed a pile of matches from her front porch and burned the letter. As the flakes of paper flew away, so did a piece of Anna's hope of finding Bill. She wanted revenge, but would it make her feel better? She wasn't sure, but she couldn't seem to let go. Not completely.

June 2062 – Present Day
Anna Faroe – The Red Rocks
Brentwood, Arizona

"What is this pose called? Dancing Shiva?" A short redhead breathed heavily on the yoga mat next to Anna. Their matching gray tank tops and leggings were sweat-stained.

"Yes, I think so," Anna replied, stepping down after losing her balance. "Damn it, Sasha, look what you made me do."

"Sorry, I'm barely holding on myself!" She laughed, wavering back and forth on one foot.

On the broad front porch of Anna's bungalow, they moved from one position to the next. The setting sun was brightening the reddish Bradshaw Mountains in front of them. Around them, the flat expanse was covered with dying yellow grass. The sky above, feathered with clouds, morphed from a loud crimson to a violent violet.

"Is it time to drink wine already?" Sasha pouted.

"No." Anna moved to the downward dog pose. "We have to lie down for five breaths and then thank ourselves for the exercise." She lowered herself onto the mat.

Sasha scoffed. "I'm not fucking doing that, but you go ahead."

Anna laughed. Typical Sasha. They had met a month ago at Andrew's Pub, a restaurant rumored to be owned by a famous Metropolitan chef who worked there in disguise. Sasha had been flirting with the bartender in hopes of getting a free drink when Anna walked in. When the bartender made up his mind to offer Sasha one, she requested one for Anna as well.

Sasha Ferriera was in her late twenties and had come to the Red Rocks five years ago, in 2057. This was the doctor's top recommendation, as her depression, delusions, and paranoia increased from the overstimulating lifestyle of the Metropolitans.

Sasha used to be top of her class, involved in extra-curricular activities and volunteering. Being a perfectionist and overachiever, she became a slave to time. Her anxiety increased from her busy schedule, and every time she went outside, the light and noise overwhelmed her. Eventually, she broke down, collapsed. That's when her parents bought her a house in Brentwood. They visited her every six months, but she hadn't been back to the Metropolitans since she came to the Red Rocks. Sasha was a client who turned into a friend.

"Where is your wine?" Sasha asked from inside the house, which had two small bedrooms and a living room, and smelled of lavender incense.

"Hold on!" Anna rolled up her mat and went in as a gray ball of fur brushed up against her.

"Look who's home." Anna bent down to pet the Russian blue, and headed over to the purple and yellow tapestry which kept the wine bar hidden.

Anna took out boiled chicken and rice and scooped them into little bowls. As she wiped the counter from spillage, her eyes fell on an empty letter holder. No letter came this month. She didn't know if it would. A part of her wanted there to be no more letters, no more waiting, no more flickers of hope ignited just to be blown out. Yet another part of her, the bit of anger that hasn't been squashed, nagged at her not to shut the door completely and to keep searching. But when will I ever be able to move on? Anna fought with her own thoughts.

"He's so adorable, is this Sage or Archik?" Sasha interrupted Anna's thoughts, motioning to the orange cat that sprinted into the room as soon as the chicken and rice bowls hit the floor.

"This is Sage. Archik is the Russian blue."

"Why do you even do favors like that? It's not your job to cat-sit for your clients."

Anna released her hair from a clip, it fell just past her chin, she'd changed it as soon as she moved to Brentwood.

"I don't mind," Anna said. The truth is she liked having the cats around. They made the house feel less empty.

Sasha poured a glass of wine and handed it up to Anna.

"Well, tell me about your non-cat-sitting clients. Is there anyone fun? Anyone interesting?"

"You know I can't tell you that," Anna said.

"Please! I'm dying to meet someone good in bed around here. Maybe I should become . . . um . . . whatever you call yourself."

"I'm a companion, and I don't sleep with all of my clients." The truth was, she wasn't as comfortable being intimate as she used to be. She tried to avoid it, but it was part of the job, and part of the healing process for some.

"You totally should sleep with all of them!" An evil grin appeared on Sasha's face.

She is so young, Anna thought, and doesn't understand. Just like Samien. Their world, when not in depths of sickness, revolves around simple future pleasures. And Anna's world, her world revolved around a burdened past.

June 2062 – Present Day
Anna Faroe – The Red Rocks
Brentwood, Arizona

Antonio sat at the piano, finishing the notes for "Fuer Elise." After settling into Brentwood, Anna had found it for cheap in hopes of learning how to play, but she never did. Several of her clients, on the other hand, had an aptitude. She learned that music therapy worked for both—the performer and the listener.

Anna touched the soft wood with her fingers, tracing the engravings on it, there was something erotic in her movements. "That was beautiful," she said.

"Not as beautiful as you." Antonio stood up and took her in his arms. He was a hefty man with long curly dark hair. He kissed her cheek, her neck, her shoulder. He slid down the one strap of her bra, and ran his fingers down her arm.

"Anna, I don't know what I—"

Smash! The window looking out onto Anna's front porch shattered into an irreplaceable number of dangerous pieces. A rock the size of a mandarin lay innocently in the middle of the mess.

Anna pushed Antonio away and walked toward her front door.

Thump! Another rock, twice the size of the first one landed on her Persian rug. "I know you're in there you bastard!" a woman's voice yelled from outside of the door.

Anna stopped walking, turned to Antonio and crossed her arms.

"Anna, she wasn't supposed to find your address, I don't know how—"

The door busted open. "What the hell are you doing here?!" A tall, thick woman shouldered her way to the center of Anna's living room, crunching the broken glass.

"Honey, I'm just here for—"

"Here for what?! You dirty piece of shit!" Rage spewed out of the woman's mouth and she turned to Anna. Her breath smelled sour. "This is her? The slut you've been coming to see? Am I not enough for you?"

So Anna *had* been right about his bruises.

"Get here, right this second! Or I swear I will mess you up so bad you won't be walking or fucking anywhere!" She shook her fist and Antonio sunk back into the corner like a frightened animal.

"Honey, I didn't mean anything by this. I love you. I just need a little peace and quiet."

"Oh don't honey me, you piece of industrial waste. Get your fucking shit together now!"

He grabbed his cardigan and walked toward his wife. He left a few Red Rock notes on Anna's coffee table and mouthed, "I'm sorry."

"And what do you have to say for yourself, you filthy whore?" The woman leaned in to Anna, her eyes were pure venom.

"Please leave. I don't want any trouble," Anna said. She had no patience for anyone who abused their partner.

"Oh I will leave alright, after I beat your blue-eyed face into a pulp so you stop stealing all our husbands!" The woman flew into Anna grabbing her hair. Anna squeezed her eyes through the pain, but didn't scream. She punched the woman in the stomach, but the woman didn't budget, weighing at least twice of Anna.

"What are you doing? I said I'll go with you. Let's go!" Antonio shouted helplessly.

"Not until she learns her lesson!" The woman's voice held a deafening pitch.

"Let go of me and get out of my house!" Anna pinched the woman's bicep. She let out a squeal, but held on.

Antonio tried to pull his wife away, but his wife elbowed him skillfully in the ribs. He doubled over.

"You're a pathetic piece of shit." She turned around, pulling Anna by her hair, and spat on him, the slimy string mingling with his curls.

"Stop it!" Anna said. "Please just leave and I won't mention this to anyone."

The woman snorted. "Who are you going to tell? I can murder your skinny little ass and bury you in the desert in pieces. You think anyone would care?"

The question made her uneasy. *I don't know.*

"Exactly, you stupid bitch. No one cares about whores." She punched Anna in the gut. Anna coughed as air slipped out of her lungs. Anna saw Antonio get up and hit his wife in the back with his fist. She winced but didn't budge.

"You little mongrel, you think you can cause me pain? You are a joke!" She prepared another punch for Anna.

Anna closed her eyes. Maybe it was a mistake to come back to this line of work. Maybe it was—

Pop! Anna heard a ligament crack and expected to feel pain, but none came.

"Ow!" The broad-shouldered wife whelped and Anna felt the grip on her hair loosen. She opened her eyes; a man was holding the wife's arms behind her back.

"Are you okay?" he asked. His eyes shone brown and green in the light.

Anna nodded.

"Did they rob you?"

"No. It was just a misunderstanding," Anna said apprehensively.

"Misunderstand my—eek!" Anna saw the handsome man tighten his hold before the wife could finish her sentence.

"With your permission, I will let her out."

"Please." Anna watched the man walk the woman to the door and slightly nudge her over the doorstep. Antonio had already made his way outside and stood several feet away past the porch. Anna gathered her messy locks up with a clip, as the handsome man closed the door.

"Would you like some tea?" Anna said and walked over to get some for herself. Pain ricocheted in her abdomen from the hit.

"Sure."

She handed him a small cup of honeyed green tea and gestured for him to sit on the piano stool as most of her other furniture sparkled with menacing shards of glass. Anna looked at him as he sipped the tea. He was older and well put together. No wrinkles on his shirt, no stains on his jeans, and yet, there was a roughness about him. His hair was short and combed to the side, and his beard was neatly trimmed.

"What brings you here today?" Anna cringed as her ribs throbbed.

"Are you okay?" he asked. "Do you want me to take a look?" He moved towards her and started to lift the bottom part of her shirt.

Anna cleared her throat.

He quickly let go, blushing. "I'm sorry, that was inappropriate."

Anna thought about everything that just happened and let out a laugh. The handsome man came in and rescued her from a crazy wife, whose husband was sneaking around with a companion. "I think out of everyone, you are the least inappropriate in this situation."

The man stayed quiet.

"Tell me. What can I do for you?" she asked.

"I'm not sure," he responded, his voice was steady, but Anna detected a nervousness underneath.

"That's okay. We can figure that out together. What is your name?"

The man studied her for a moment before responding, as if deciding whether to stay or go. "Dustin," he finally said.

"Thank you for saving me Dustin," Anna said. "I can't promise that if we spend time together the days will be as adventurous as today."

"Adventure is overrated."

July 2062 – Present Day
Anna Faroe – The Red Rocks
Brentwood, Arizona

Anna lay on the couch in her living room. It was hot and she had no more batteries left for her personal fan. She kept a luke-warm water bowl next to her and sprinkled herself every couple of minutes. A nice day to myself, she thought, but her mind kept wandering back to Bobby's last letter.

They had a lead, they must've been close, she thought. But now nothing for two months? They must've lost his trace, or maybe they found him and . . . I can't keep thinking about this. I need to try to get back to my calm, balanced self. At least until another letter comes.

Anna sat up and picked up a magazine she bought from the book store. She thought it would help her focus on something else besides finding Bill. She flipped to an article that talked about the exploitation of young women and men. There was a new popular life-subscriber campaign where you wear a thin layer of ad strips on your body, and other people subscribe to your life, watching your every move, every action, every breath—from any angle they choose. She threw the magazine in the trash.

Organizing always helps me keep my mind clear, she thought, and walked over to her red oak bookshelf. She took all of the books out and began putting them back in alphabetical order by genre. She was so engrossed in the process that she didn't hear the little bell ring when the door to her house creaked open.

"Hi," said a familiar deep voice, it held a hint of excitement. "Am I interrupting?"

"No." She smoothed out her shirt. "I didn't think I'd see you again," she said. Dustin had left abruptly last time. She guessed he was new to being with a companion. A small part of her was glad to see him again after these two weeks. Something about him piqued her interest.

He looked into her eyes, she noticed the touch of green in them grew bright. "I'm sorry about the other night, I—"

"There's no need to explain."

"I should go," he said.

Anna stood up. "Please stay. We don't need to do anything. We can just talk."

Dustin looked at the door, and then looked back at her. He didn't say anything.

"Would you like something to drink?"

He smoothed out his beard and nodded. "Whiskey, if you have it." He sat on the couch, placing his hands between his knees.

She walked over with the drinks and they sat looking at each other for some time. *It will take time to get to know him*, she thought. *He's searching for something—or maybe someone. I'll have to be the one that breaks the ice.*

"You have an eyelash on one of your cheeks," she said.

"Which cheek?"

"It's better if you guess."

"I don't like to guess."

"If you guess correctly, then you get to make a wish."

"Is that so?" he said, amused.

Anna nodded. "That's what I hear."

"Okay," he said. "Right."

Anna smiled. "The wish is yours," she said.

Dustin tried to get the eyelash off his cheek.

"Let me." Anna cupped her hand around his face and wiped his cheek with her thumb. Their eyes locked. He leaned in, but then pulled back.

July 2062 – Present Day
Dustin Thorne – The Red Rocks
Brentwood, Arizona

Dustin stood outside his hotel, smoking. He left Anna's place feeling anxious, and went to clear his mind. She was nice, and there was an attraction, but it was very strange to pay. He wasn't sure if this was right for him—if he was ready. But are you ever? he thought.

He flicked the lit cigarette in the street and went into the southwestern style building, which has become his home. There were six private rooms, a small bar, and a dining hall. His room was neat and quiet. He sat down on his bed and opened the book he had been reading; his boot tapped the wooden floor as he stared down at the pages. He finally closed it, unable to concentrate, and looked outside his window. Across from him, was another hotel, a flower pot stood on the windowsill. Inside the pot, a single poppy grew, it danced to the rhythm of the wind. It reminded him of Anna—beautiful, but lonely. Should I go back and see her again? he wondered.

~ ~ ~

Two days later, Dustin led his horse down Main Street. The streets were unusually busy, impeding his way. It was hard to squeeze through the scores of people. I can always turn back, he thought, but knew that he wouldn't.

He reached Anna's house just as a hooded man was riding away. Another client? Dustin thought, or someone else? When he got closer, he saw that she was holding a letter.

"Mail from a faraway friend?" he asked.

Anna jumped back, startled. "I didn't see you there," she said. "Please give me a moment." She tucked the letter under her arm and went inside, not giving him an answer to his question.

Perhaps she's not expecting pleasant news, he thought. Perhaps this wasn't a good idea.

"Now, a proper hello." Anna reappeared looking radiant in a low-cut tank top and a pair of jeans. She gave him a peck on the cheek, and Dustin relaxed a bit.

"So where are we going?" Anna asked.

"Do you trust me?" Dustin responded.

"Trust is overrated," Anna teased, mimicking his comment about adventure, from the first time they met. He laughed to himself, and any doubts he had left about seeing her, dissipated.

They rode in silence, the warm wind embracing them. At the far end of town, they stopped next to a building whose paint was having a hard time holding on. Dustin took Anna's hand as they walked through the door. An empty room lit only by the afternoon sun, striving to make its way through the windows, welcomed them. An old guitar stood in the corner, and Dustin walked over to it.

"Are you going to serenade me?" she asked, her blue eyes sparkling with amusement.

"If you let me," he replied, a playfulness behind his words. Then he took a deep breath, and said, "You know, for a while, I couldn't play my guitar."

Anna looked at him, her knowing eyes urging him to continue.

"I started again, not too long ago," Dustin said, after a moment.

"And how did it feel, to start again after all this time?" Anna asked, her raven hair fell across her eyes.

"It took some time, but now, it's like I never stopped."

Anna sat down on a rickety chair in the corner of the room, as Dustin strummed the chords. A sad melody, intertwined with notes of hope. After he finished, he took out a champagne bottle and two flutes.

Anna's face lit up. "I haven't had champagne in years."

Dustin brought his flute up. "To fun surprises."

"To new beginnings," Anna responded.

After finishing their drinks, they slow-danced to the silence. He pulled her in and kissed her.

I can't rush this, he thought, and drew back.

August 2062 – Present Day
Anna Faroe – The Red Rocks
Brentwood, Arizona

"Let's go to the stage!" Anna shouted above the crowd. Dustin shook his head, reluctantly. She snapped his suspenders which was the only costume piece she had convinced him to wear. She, herself, wore a barmaid's dress for this impromptu Andrew's Pub Beer Fest that she and Sasha, who they lost hours ago, had been invited to.

Anna pulled Dustin with her through the mass of people toward the loud metal music roaring from the stage. Fists went up and down in the air, some brushing the low ceiling. The smell of fried food created a feeling of comfort, sending grumbling bellies to stand in long lines for overpriced hamburgers.

Dustin had been coming to see her for a month. He was a nice contrast to her younger clients. He planned outings and brought her gifts—rare wines, chocolates, cheeses. He was a strong man, but a private man. He intrigued her. A man of few words, she thought, not like . . . She stopped herself before her thoughts continued down a path she could not come back from, and fixed her attention on Dustin, who looked like he was having fun jumping up and down next to the bass player.

"Ouch!" A stout bearded man plummeted down on her foot. "Can you move?" she yelled.

"If you can't handle it, you shouldn't be up here!" The man shrugged, sweat pouring down his face.

"You're an asshole!" Anna said, and moved a step away from him.

"You're a cunt that can't handle her shit obviously!" He bumped her with his meaty thigh, making her stumble.

"What did you say?" Dustin's deep voice skated above the music. He stood tall in front of Anna. People around them backed away.

"None of your business." The man's bushy eyebrows moved toward his nose.

"Apologize to the lady," Dustin demanded.

"She's no lady." The man grinned, looking down Anna's dress.

"Say that again," Dustin pressed a finger into the man's chest. The man stayed quiet. "Apologize, now."

"I don't think so." The man made a chunky fist and swung at Dustin, who ducked and cracked him in the jaw sending him staggering backwards. The music stopped, and two men in charge of security ran over.

"What's going on here?" They asked, hands on their guns. They were both short, and their muscles pushed through their skinny white tank tops.

"We were just leaving," Dustin said and jumped off stage, helping Anna down. "You better hope we never run into each other again," he warned. A growl came from where the stout man stood.

As they walked out, they heard one of the security men say, "You too, asshole. Get the fuck out."

When the door shut behind them, Dustin asked, "You okay?"

"I'm okay," Anna said. "Thank you for that."

Dustin nodded. They walked down the hot, noisy street in silence, and then ducked into Dustin's hotel to save themselves from the sun's unforgiving rays. They went into the bar section, and sat down on the velvet couch in the corner.

Anna felt good. It was nice to feel protected, to feel taken care of. "You brought me back to something I haven't felt for a long time," Anna said.

"And what is that?"

"A moment of feeling that everything might turn out okay in the end."

"Only a moment?"

"That's what life is, isn't it? A series of moments? Each one with the potential to make your life infinitely better or infinitely worse?

"And how did my moment score from a scale of one to ten, with ten being infinitely better?"

"I'd say a five." Anna held his hand.

"Only a five?" Dustin frowned, but underneath a smile lingered. "What can I do to make it at least a six?"

"What do you think you should do?"

Dustin's hand moved down her waist and his lips brushed her cheek. They kissed, the heat of their bodies rising. He took the glass out of her hand and set it down, then stood and picked her up, and she wrapped her legs tightly around him. He carried her upstairs to his room and pressed her against the wall. She flung off her shirt, and Dustin's mouth and hands caught her breasts as they tumbled out. She sighed as his hand moved lower down her body; her nails dug into his skin.

He took off her panties and his lips found her as she ran her fingers through his hair. She couldn't hold on any longer, she pulled him up and they fell on the bed. Their moans grew louder and Anna arched her back in pleasure as Dustin's body tensed and released, dropping down onto her—their bodies wet, their breathing heavy.

They lay on the sheets, feeling each other's nakedness, enjoying the silence. It was the first time they were intimate, and she didn't want to move, as if not to scare the moment away. She had a feeling Dustin felt the same.

~ ~ ~

The next day, Anna came home to find a letter on her doorstep. She didn't need to open it to know who it was from. *Bobby.* The last message she had received was again, empty of hope, but she felt this time would be different. She held the letter in her hands. It felt heavier than the previous ones. She slid her fingers across it and took a deep breath. She made a small rip, but then stopped and put the letter in a cabinet. Today, she didn't want any news; her mind was somewhere else. Today, her mind was with Dustin.

September 2062 – Present Day
Dustin Thorne – The Red Rocks
Brentwood, Arizona

Anna lay in Dustin's arms on the bed in his hotel. It was three months since they first met, and they had grown close. He felt comfortable with her. He felt like he could open up to her. Perhaps one day he would.

"Were you watching me sleep?" she said, looking up at him.

Dustin replied with a half-smile. His dark eyes prominent in the morning light.

She squinted at him. "Your eyes, they look nice, they look darker."

He tilted his head. "I wear contacts sometimes"—Dustin paused—"to entice beautiful women into my bed."

Anna laughed. "Where are all of these beautiful women?"

"I got you, didn't I? You're not going to leave me now that you know my eye color secret, are you?" Dustin joked.

"You have nice eyes, but that's not why I'm dating you."

Dating, Dustin noted. "Anna, I'd like to take you away for a few weeks."

"Oh really? You want me all to yourself?"

"I do." Dustin caressed her shoulder.

"Do I have a choice?"

"Only the illusion of one." Dustin blocked a playful kick from Anna.

"I think it could be possible." She traced a scar on his chest.

"Will there be issues with your clients if you take time off?"

Anna raised a thin, curved eyebrow. "Men usually don't like to talk about my clients."

Dustin didn't either, but he knew better than to ask her to sacrifice her job for him. It's better if she decides to leave her clients herself, Dustin thought. He didn't respond to her comment, knowing it would prompt her to continue.

"I can clear my schedule for a few weeks. I only have a few clients left. They seem to come and go quickly in this town. Where would we go?"

"Vegas."

September 2062 – Present Day
Anna Faroe – The Red Rocks
Road to Las Vegas, Arizona

Anna and Dustin had been on the road for three days and were almost halfway to Vegas. Her thoughts kept coming back to Bobby's letter. She took it with her, but did not open it. She was afraid that if she did, she'd get pulled back to her memories of Jake. To how much she loved him and to how much she wished that his murderer got what he deserved. She wanted to let go completely, but she couldn't.

Once more, Anna pushed these thoughts away and tried to focus on the surroundings: the terrain, vast and empty, but not silent; the sky, covered in heavy-bellied clouds ready to burst at any moment.

All of a sudden she was enveloped in a thick tornado of dust and her horse started galloping at an incredible speed.

Anna couldn't see anything in front or behind her and screamed. Her horse, confused, reared, and Anna fell on her back, getting her breath knocked out of her.

"Anna!" She heard Dustin's voice, but couldn't see. She closed her eyes and opened them to find him inches away from her on the ground. He placed his bandana on her face, and then covered her body with his.

Dust and dirt whirled around them and tumbleweeds marched in a scratchy brigade. They were surrounded. She tried to breathe and choked. Her lungs burned and she pressed her body harder against his.

"Don't worry, I got you," Dustin whispered. He held her tight, his lips touching the top of her head. His breath was slow, calculated, and she followed his lead. Breathe in, breathe out, in and out, Anna coached herself—it helped her stay calm. And then, moments later, it was over— the air clear and welcoming, as if nothing had happened.

They didn't speak as they stood up, both caked in dust— two desert mummies. She felt fragile, suffocated by the re-occurring thought that everything in life was temporary, and that in one instance, her whole world could be turned upside down. She petted her horse and cleaned her up with water from her canteen. Maybe this was a sign, a sign for her to finally let go of the past. Not forget, but let go, and focus on the present—on living each day, each minute, each second.

"We should get going, I know a place where we'll be protected from the wind," Dustin said.

"Okay," Anna responded. Dustin was her present. Dustin was good for her. He made her feel loved, he made her feel safe. He made her feel like she could move on.

~ ~ ~

Hours later, Dustin and Anna were relaxing in the tent, after eating bread and hard cheese. Anna's head was in the crook of Dustin's arm, and he was stroking her hair. Rain pattered the hide of their tent with a hypnotic beat. The sweet smell of wet earth mixed with the odor of their bodies. The inside of the tent felt warm and moist—it was strangely comforting, like a mother's womb.

"What a night, I'm glad we stopped when we did." Anna snuggled closer to Dustin.

"This doesn't bother you, does it?" She could see his breath as he spoke.

"What? The travel?" She looked up at him, her blue eyes tired.

"It's not always easy for people that don't ride often."

"Just because I don't, doesn't mean I don't like to."

"But you don't," he said and pulled her close.

Anna patted the sleeping bag underneath them. "I would be lying if I said I like sleeping on the cold ground more than I do in my own bed, but I like being with you."

Dustin smiled. "You remind me of . . ."

"Of what?"

"Of my first love."

Anna shifted her position. She liked that he was letting her in.

"What was she like?" Anna asked.

"Do you really want to know?"

"Yes," Anna said. "She was a big part of your life, and I want to get to know everything about you, if you let me."

Dustin nodded, thoughtfully. "Okay," he said and popped open a bottle of brandy they bought from a couple of travelers they'd met on the road. "She was idealistic, opinionated, and wild." He took a swallow. "But she was also, perfect."

"What happened to her?"

"She died." He coughed. "It was unfair how it happened. I blamed myself for a long time," he said and smoothed out his beard. "One night we had a fight. It was a stupid fight . . . about having kids. I was pushing her to start thinking about a baby, about changing our lives, our habits. She didn't want to, she said she was too young, and she liked the way things were." He paused, then shook his head. "I should've told her to stay, but she was so angry. She stormed out . . ."

Anna laced her fingers through his and squeezed them lightly. She felt his pain. She knew it all too well.

Dustin looked away. "She never came back. She was attacked. A random robbery."

"I'm so sorry," Anna said.

"I spent years hating myself, going over every word of our fight. Why was I so pushy? Why did I even care about the damn kids? What should I have said to make her stay?"

"Do you still go over it?"

"Yes. But for the first time in a long time, I feel like I've made my peace with it. And you're helping me hold on to that feeling."

Anna lifted herself to give him a kiss. "Do you still think about having kids?"

"I do," Dustin said. "And you?"

"I'm not sure," Anna said. "I was pregnant once before . . ."

Dustin stayed quiet and stroked her hair.

"I was in a destructive relationship when I was young. One where no matter what you do, or how bad everything gets, you keep coming back." A flash of lightning brightened their tent, and seconds later, thunder clapped.

Dustin handed Anna the brandy. "How did you get out of it?"

"I didn't. He left me after he found out I was pregnant. I ended up miscarrying." Anna took a tiny sip. "It's not uncommon to miscarry, but after, they told me that I probably wouldn't be able to have another child. It's a strange feeling when that choice is taken away from you, even if it's not something you think you want." Dustin nodded. This time it was his turn to squeeze her hand.

September 2062 – Present Day
Anna Faroe – The Red Rocks
Sterling, Arizona

Anna was lying on the hotel bed, writing in her notebook. They had decided to stop in the small town of Sterling to get some rest and get cleaned up. She looked around the room—the walls were bare except for a lonely painting of an orange tree. It looked celestial, its branches offering the sweetest fruit, but there was no one to accept it. She looked back down at her notebook, and flipped to a photo of Jake. *Are you happy for me . . . that I'm moving on?*

"What are you writing about?" Dustin asked.

Anna cleared her throat. "Just thoughts and some of our travel stories. I don't want to forget anything." She smiled.

"Will you read me some of it?" Dustin held her gaze with his dark eyes.

"Maybe." She put down the notebook. "But later." She moved closer to him on the bed and drew him in with a kiss.

Elizabeth Povarova-Simpson

September 2062 – Present Day
Dustin Thorne – The Red Rocks
Sterling, Arizona

    Dustin woke up at midday and saw that Anna was out. He found his briefs tangled in the covers and slid them on. When he picked up his jeans, something shifted underneath. It was Anna's notebook. He lifted it and read:

> You'll always have a piece of my heart, Jake, and I will always carry a small piece of you with me.

    Above the words was a photograph of a young man with bright green eyes and tangled hair. He took a closer look, then went to the bathroom and threw up.

November 2061 ~ 10 Months Ago
Bill Vos – The Red Rocks
Alena, Arizona

Bill sat in a bar, hundreds of miles away from Livingsworth, thousands of moments from the life he had seven months ago. Bill looked into his glass, a distorted reflection of a bearded man stared back at him. He rubbed his eyes, dried out from the contacts that added green to his dark irises. This was a nice town. Perhaps he'd stay here for a few weeks.

Alena was the fifth town he had visited, after six months of camping in the middle of the desert. During that time, he had fought through the pain of losing everyone close to him. He hadn't been sure how he would go on. He mourned his mother-in-law, and he mourned Jake.

When he found out his mother-in-law passed away, he felt upset, and yet a strange sense of closure came over him. He had fulfilled his promise to Emmy, he had done his best to take care of her family. Now, with no one left, he could move forward with his life. *I'm no longer the man you used to know, Emmy, or the man I used to know. I'm someone else. I want to leave all of this behind.*

Jake was harder to mourn. A friend. An unlikely accident. He buried the memory in the deepest part of his soul and comforted himself with the thought that it wasn't his fault. He had to think this way, or there would be no tomorrow. The guilt would swallow him up.

A young, light-haired waitress came up to him. "Here you go." She handed him a guitar.

"Thank you." Bill unbuttoned the cuffs on his shirt, rolled up his sleeves and tugged on the strings. The sounds morphed into a pleasant melody. It was the first time he played since Emmy died.

"You're really good, what's your name?" the waitress asked after he was done.

He gave her a half-smile. "Dustin Thorne."

September 2062 – Present Day
Bill Vos – The Red Rocks
Sterling, Arizona

Bill looked at himself in the bathroom mirror, his face was pale and body slick with sweat. He heard the hotel room door open and close. *Knock. Knock. Knock.*

"Hey! I brought us some coffee and sandwiches. Your favorite—a spreadable meat paste I cannot recognize and possibly moldy cheese," Anna joked.

Bill felt a second round of vomit creeping up his throat. "Thanks. I'll be right out."

He took a deep breath. Did she know? His whole body shook. No, she couldn't; she would've killed him by now. He put his head in his hands and sat down on the covered toilet bucket. The right thing to do was to leave right now. Let her be, and let himself be. He washed his face in the basin, brushed his hair, and wiped the sweat off with a towel.

September 2062 – Present Day
Anna Faroe – The Red Rocks
Road to Las Vegas, Nevada

Two days later they were still on the road to Vegas. They journeyed in silence, though Anna tried to make small talk. On day three, they saw an abandoned shack, the type you see on a long desert road, in the middle of nowhere. They checked for supplies and found water and canned soup and beans. Dustin also came across a latch to a hidden floor compartment, which contained several bottles of whiskey. A tiny mouse skull and bones lay beside them.

Poor thing, Anna thought. It probably got in there by accident, and when it wanted to leave, it was too late—the door was closed. She sighed.

Anna felt tired. Her lips flaked from dryness; her sunburned skin craved moisture. She watched Dustin lay out dried fruit and meat on the bar in the shack. He stayed quiet and Anna felt his discontent.

"What's been on your mind?" They were sitting on cracked wooden stools, drinking their newly found goods.

The smooth and smoky taste was pleasant and felt warm going down.

"Nothing." Dustin ran his fingers through his hair.

"Something is wrong. I can feel it." Anna said and hopped off her stool. She walked over to him, put her hands on his legs, and leaned in to kiss him. Slowly, she unbuttoned his top shirt button, and then nuzzled his neck.

Dustin pulled away. "I think we'd better save our strength for the road." He looked off to the side and took a sip of whiskey.

September 2062 – Present Day
Bill Vos – The Red Rocks
Road to Las Vegas, Nevada

I have to let her go, Bill thought, as he watched Anna sleep. He kissed her on the lips. She mumbled and turned around, covering her head with the blanket. If he was going to leave, then he needed to leave now. He looked out and saw the sun peeking through the early morning fog.

They had set up camp outside the shack. He had used cooling foil to keep their tent from overheating; it would last several more hours.

He gathered his clothes, his gear, and took a few Red Rocks pellets for himself, leaving most for Anna. He left her almost all of his Red Rock notes, and a gun for protection. He knew he needed to tell her something, but he couldn't tell her who he was. She'd hate him. She'd hate herself. Even though he had fallen in love with her, if she knew the truth, she wouldn't be able to love him back. He wrote down his words carefully:

> I have to go. I cannot tell you why, but trust my decision that this is right. Don't try to find me. It's best for both of us that we never see each other again.

Bill folded the note and left it underneath her canteen. He turned around one last time to look at her, she was peaceful and gave out a tiny snore which made him smile.

He went to get his horse; she was tied to a dead palm tree, one of many that invaded the flat terrain. As he prepped her, he heard what sounded like four pairs of hooves.

A minute later, a scream wailed from the direction of their tent. Bill ran toward it to find one man standing outside.

"Young and precious," uttered a slurred voice from inside the tent. "What a fine piece of ass to find on such an early morning."

"Get out!?" Anna's cry was dulled by the walls of thick hide and foil.

The man outside the tent saw Bill coming and fumbled to take out his gun.

"Get off! Don't touch me!" Anna yelled.

"Don't come any closer." The man in front of the tent had a scar across his face that ran from his missing left eye down to the corner of his mouth.

"Tell your man to get the fuck off of her." Bill's voice rang out loud and clear.

"Oh, we have a boy protector here." The other man appeared out from the tent. He had a crooked nose—one that has been broken many times.

"You want to play?" One-eye said and cocked his gun.

Bill sidestepped and kicked the gun out of One-eye's hand. Crooked-nose jumped up and wrapped his arms around Bill from the back. Bill used him as a wall and bounced back, kicking One-eye in the chest.

"Go Anna, get out of here!" Bill instructed, and Crooked-nose, still holding onto Bill, used one arm to take out his knife and slice Bill down his back. He grunted but did not fall; instead he kicked the man behind him in the knee with his heel.

"I won't leave you," Anna said.

Crooked-nose yelped and squatted to the ground as Bill kicked him again.

In front of Bill, One-eye tried to regain his balance and scramble for the gun, but Anna ran up to him to push it away and he kicked her in the chest. She cried out and fell. Bill tried to run to her, but Crooked-nose pushed him and he hit the hard dirt facedown.

"Anna, run if you can," Bill pleaded. He felt a boot on his back and lost his breath. One-eye was nearing Anna, but she crawled away into the tent.

"You snooty bitch!" The one-eyed man followed her while Crooked-nose hit Bill in the side while he was down.

The Red Rocks

Bill retrieved the knife in his boot and stabbed Crooked-nose through the foot.

"Fuuuuck!" the man spat out and hopped off.

"I'm coming to get you, you bitch!" One-eye called.

Boom! One-eye staggered backwards. Blood spilled from his gut. "Dustin!" Anna ran out of the tent, still holding the gun she used to shoot One-eye.

"We have to get out of here," Bill said.

"You're hurt," she said, running her fingers down his sliced shirt.

"I'll be okay. We need to go," he said. "We can leave everything here, I have extra supplies with me."

When they were far enough away from the intruders, they planted themselves beneath the first shade they could find. Bill looked at Anna, and she at him. Then he ripped off her shirt, taking in her beauty, and kissed her roughly. They wrapped themselves in each other, dirty, bloody—raw.

~ ~ ~

While Anna slept, Bill went back to the tent. He took water, dried meat, Anna's bag of clothing, and recovered the note he had left. There was an envelope on the floor of the tent, next to Anna's notebook. It was a sealed letter. He opened it up to find a sketch of himself and a note. It read:

> We found him. I'm sending men out to get him. I only beg you that if you see him, stay away from him. He is a dangerous man and Jake would want you to be safe. I will write again once I hear back from the bounty hunters.

Bill burned both his note and the letter, and then walked back to Anna.

September 2062 – Present Day
Anna Faroe – The Red Rocks
Las Vegas, Nevada

After two days of recovering and healing their wounds, they were back on the road. I'm so glad we're almost there, Anna thought, and yet something tugged at her heart. She couldn't quite put her finger on what was bothering her. She thought part of it was that she couldn't find the letter from Bobby. It should have been in her notebook, which she had found, but when she looked through it, there was no letter tucked away between the pages. She pushed the uneasiness away.

As they neared the city, Anna could see broken-down trailers, giant tents, and rusty vans forming mini-clusters of vagrant camps. They grew in density as they got closer and closer to the city.

"What's that?" Anna pointed at the faint green, red, and yellow lights shooting from the city center.

"That is the use of stolen electricity."

"Stolen electricity?" She was glad to switch her attention away from her worry and relaxed as Dustin responded.

"Vegas gets its electricity by hacking into power grids. I don't know all of the details, but I'm sure we can ask someone when we get there."

"What about marshals? Isn't this illegal?"

"They get paid to take a route inside the city that bypasses all the unwarranted activities." Dustin turned to her with a grin.

Feverish excitement rushed over her. "So are there radios? TVs?" She loved to watch movies when she lived back in the Metropolitans; the thought of seeing one again for the first time in years made her feel the bittersweet ache of nostalgia.

"Yes. It's not the way it used to be right before 08/06/2040, since they can't steal that much electricity from the State, but it sure is more than anywhere else in the Red Rocks."

Her eyes lit up. She looked at Dustin—strong, handsome, kind, smart. She couldn't even remember what she was worried about in the first place.

"There it is." Dustin pointed ahead. The spears and rectangles of buildings flooded the city horizon. She was happy to be here, and happy to be with him.

September 2062 – Present Day
Bill Vos – The Red Rocks
Las Vegas, Nevada

They arrived at dusk. The city looked divine—an angelic blanket covering the devil's playground. It looked alive already, or maybe alive still? The streets were overwhelmed with people—some laughing, some crying, some carrying illegal smiles. From one casino door to the next, was a slowly moving line, only interrupted by fights for bike taxis.

They stood next to a closed-down casino at the edge of the city, peeking into this strange wonderland.

"Let's go." Bill jumped off his horse and helped Anna down from hers.

"This is something else." Anna took off her hat, letting her hair fall free.

"I knew you'd like it." Bill took her hand and pointed to where a man was walking by in a pink bunny costume, holding the hand of a woman in a gold leotard, top hat, and cape.

Bill offered his half-smile. "Welcome to Vegas."

~ ~ ~

In their hotel room, Bill and Anna soaked in neighboring bathtubs. The water had turned brown as soon as they got in, exhausted, relieved.

"I never told you this," Anna began, her voice coarse from the ride. "But until about a year ago, I've only lived in one other town in the Red Rocks."

"And where would that be?" he asked, hoping that maybe she wasn't Jake's Anna after all, and he had hallucinated the picture of Jake in the notebook.

"It's a town up north, called Livingsworth." Anna ran her finger along the edge of the porcelain tub.

Bill closed his eyes tight, trying to propel the dark memories of Jake away. There is no way to change what happened, Bill thought. I need to figure out what to do, sooner rather than later. I can either tell her, or I can leave, or . . .

Bill tensed as his mind fought within. For the first time since Emmy, I found someone I care just as deeply for. I love her. Bill felt a longing inside.

"I wanted to thank you, Dustin. Thank you for bringing me here, and not just here, but on the road, showing me the things I never would have seen."

He looked at her and she was radiant—dripping wet hair, soft skin, blue eyes. She's happy, Bill thought. That's what matters. "Anna?"

"Yes?" An upward curve at the corner of her lips.

"I need to tell you something."

September 2062 – Present Day
Anna Faroe – The Red Rocks
Las Vegas, Nevada

Anna got out of her bath and walked over to Dustin, her heart a turbine in the wind. She bent down and looked him in his eyes.

"I'm falling in love with you too." She smiled and pulled him out of his bath.

Dustin stood inches away, towering over her, bringing her even closer as he put his chin on her head. "I want you to know that I will spend every day doing my best to make you happy."

~ ~ ~

It was the fourth day since they had arrived, and the last three they had spent sleeping, eating, and relaxing in their cozy little room. The walls were painted a light green, and across the bed hung a painting of a T.V. The back of the painting listed the top locations in Vegas where you can go watch television. Anna felt it was time for them to visit one of those places.

She looked out the foggy hotel window. "The weather looks like it won't be as hot today. What do you say? Shall we go out on the town?"

"Today is the perfect day to go," Dustin said, walking up behind her and embracing her with his muscular arms. "With you, every day is perfect." Anna was glad that Dustin was more relaxed since the moment he told her that he loved her. Her uneasiness, too, had subsided.

Outside, the sun ricocheted off of all the casino walls, some standing strong, others crumbling. They walked across the street and watched fountains dance to classical music in front of the largest casino in Vegas, luring even the most eager gambler to stop and observe. When they walked inside, they were hit with a wave of cigarette smoke. The golden glare from the card suit wall décor was blinding, and the noise of coins dropping from the old-fashioned slot machines was deafening. Anna remembered her grandparents telling her that there was nothing like the feeling of coins raining down in a rich waterfall, filling up your bucket. Her grandparents loved to come to Vegas, but they always told *her* to stay away. It was a cruel and dangerous place, they'd say. It won't be for me, Anna thought. For me, it will be good.

"How about we play some Black Jack." Anna pointed to a table with a barrel-chested dealer, his suspenders one tense move away from busting.

"Hey there." He rolled up his sleeves. "Ready to play?"

"It's been a while, but I think I'm ready to take a chance." She turned to Dustin, who threw a hundred on the table.

"How much will you bet?" asked Dustin.

"All in," she said.

~ ~ ~

Three hours, seven cocktails, and five hundred Red Rock notes later, they sat in a small crowded room, eating popcorn and drinking bourbon. In front of them, stood a television set playing a VCR tape. The movie was a 1980s flick about a car that could go into the future. The place played three movies per show. Between the movies, performers would come out—each one known for a special talent. One girl did a routine on an aerial rope, another dancer came out and crushed a full can of beer between her breasts, and then a man with a shirt that said "Big D" came out and did fifty backflips.

"Let's try our luck at this place," said Dustin, handing Anna the cash and pointing to the mini slot machine on the way out of the fake theater.

"You still believe I'll bring you luck, even after tonight?" Anna twirled a loose strand of hair around her finger.

"I'll always believe in you, no matter what," Dustin said.

Anna stuck the coin in and pulled the lever, the rolls stopped at three sevens and a hundred coins fell out. She and Dustin both jumped up and hugged each other.

"I can't believe that we are here. This all feels like a dream. I feel so close to you, like I've known you all of my life," said Anna, shivering, although it wasn't cold. "You are so good," she continued. "I feel like I don't deserve you."

Dustin enveloped her in his arms. "Believe me," he said. "It's me who doesn't deserve you."

~ ~ ~

Several hours later, after losing half of what they had won and eating a questionable, yet delicious street hamburger, Anna and Dustin were on their way back to the hotel.

"Hey look!" Anna pointed to a dirt-spotted sign in an alley.

"Storyteller," Dustin observed.

Anna grabbed his hand and pulled him into the tiny dark street filled with empty alcohol containers and cigarette packs.

A small man with faded blue eyes sat in front of a stained door. He wore a heavy coat despite the hot weather. "Are you here for a story? I know many." He smiled, showing that half of his teeth were gone.

"How about you tell us a story of your choice?" Dustin said.

"It doesn't work that way," he said and spat on the ground.

Anna looked at Dustin and shrugged. "How about the story of Las Vegas?"

"You're close," the man said, "but the one you want to hear is *your* story of Las Vegas."

"Okay." Anna agreed.

"Vegas can make people think they are someone else, believe they can manipulate fate, even love their enemies," the man began, a manic glimmer in his eyes. "But one does not know the real truth, the secrets this big city holds. Secrets of failure, secrets of love, secrets of betrayal. The travesties humankind has put upon this earth are hidden here, and sometimes they come out." He looked at both of them, then closed his eyes and rubbed his hands together in finger-less gloves. "Your story reminds me of the two that re-founded this city after its fall in 8/6/2040. A handsome man and a beautiful woman walked by the city when it was cold, dim, all the lights out. They, too, had decided to sneak away from the ads of the Metros (Metropolitans), unaware that the city they had once loved had become no more interesting than a bale of hay." He lit a cigarette and inhaled deeply, then he continued, "They were both hackers by profession, so they decided to reopen the best city in the world, but not to the way it was in recent years before they took away its juice, but to the way it was when it first bloomed.

It took them a year, but they coded and coded and finally were able to hack into a power grid and create a program which turns on the non-working turbines and generators for several hours during the day. Now the problem was to get the electricity to the city. The lovers were so excited and hyped on their dream that other people were drawn in—people who helped them trickle in the electricity. But then"—the man chewed a piece of dry skin off his lip and spat on the ground; Anna's eyes grew as she listened, taking in each word—"but then, a few weeks later, when everything was running and Vegas was 'reopened,' the man found out that the woman wasn't who she said she was, but an undercover marshal."

"What did she do?" Anna shifted from one foot to the other. Something about the story made her uncomfortable. "What did she do?" she asked again.

"It's not what she did, it's what the man did when he found out . . . he sliced her throat."

"Okay," Dustin said, irritably, and tried to pull Anna away. She stopped him.

"You're a strange man." Anna shook her head at the storyteller. "You'd make more money telling people nicer stories." She handed him two Red Rock notes.

"I only tell the truth and I'm not strange, I'm from a different world." He hacked and tucked the bills into his jacket.

"The truth will always come out in this city. If you're not who you say you are, here is where it will come to light!"

Anna frowned at the words and was about to say something when Dustin said, "Enough of this nonsense!" Then he pulled harder on her arm and they left.

October 2062 – Present Day
Bill Vos – The Red Rocks
Las Vegas, Nevada

Bill and Anna explored the city inside and out—from fancy restaurants where they could barely afford appetizers, to hidden dive bars that would write patrons' hotel room information on their backs in case they got lost on the way home.

Burlesque shows, roof top raves, T.V. clubs—they did it all, but after two weeks they decided they needed a break. Bill had suggested they switch hotels to a location father away from the center. The room they chose was small and quaint, and the view of the skyline was excellent.

One evening, they sat outside on the balcony, tall buildings staring back at them. The stars began to tease the sky—

a sparkle here, a twinkle there. Bill watched Anna, as her blue eyes inhaled the remnants of the disappearing light. She looked at him, and he embraced her. This is my reason for living, he thought. Making her happy is the only thing that's important. And she *is* happy.

"Look!" Anna pointed at a golden flicker—a shooting star, a sign of luck. That moment was perfect, it was a moment that made your life infinitely better. He wanted more moments like it.

"What did you wish for?" she asked.

"I can't tell you," Bill said. "But perhaps you'll find out soon." He knew it was crazy, but it felt right, and it was time.

November 2062 – Present Day
Anna Faroe – The Red Rocks
Las Vegas, Nevada

When Anna woke up from her nap, the clock read 6:00 P.M., later than she had wanted. Dustin had left to run errands earlier in the day. Their relationship grew this past month. It grew so much that she made the decision to stay in Las Vegas and had sent letters to her clients notifying them that she won't be coming back anytime soon. She received a letter back from Samien; he moved back home. A letter from Sasha came as well; she said she missed Anna, but was supportive of her decision, as long as that's what Anna wanted. It was.

She lazily laid in bed looking at the pale wallpaper painted with soft yellow leaves. They fell one by one, in a pattern that never reached the shaggy floor. A velvet chair stood in the corner across from the bed, a gold-plated coffee table next to it. The room spoke of tranquility, and yet, it urged for subtle action. Anna stretched and leaned over to her nightstand where she found a note. It read:

> I have a surprise for you. Get ready and walk outside. There will be a taxi waiting, he'll be holding your name on a sign. He'll take you to me. Can't wait to see you. I love you.

Anna's stomach fluttered. Each day with him brought something new. She washed her face and put on a new dress, smoothing down the soft black fabric. She paired it with black stiletto heels and a silk wrap. Why am I so nervous? she thought, noticing her hand shake as she applied mascara to her feathery lashes, and red gloss to her lips. What does he have planned? She smiled as she put her hair up, leaving a few dark locks free to complement her face.

She did a final twirl in front of the mirror, sprayed on her strawberry perfume, and walked out toward the taxis. She blushed as both men and women turned to stare when she passed by them.

"Hello, my lady." A well-dressed man standing in front of a regal blue horse carriage bowed, and helped her step inside.

They rode in silence, which made Anna tense and excited at the same time, as she guessed at what was about to happen. It seemed like hours before they reached their destination.

"Here you are, miss." The coachman helped her step down and walked her to the front of the restaurant where another man, dressed in a butler's outfit, held the door open and motioned for her to come in.

Anna took a deep breath and stepped inside to find a room filled with a hundred candles. There was a pathway of rose petals leading to a stage on the other side of the restaurant. On the stage, was a lone table, set for two. The walls around had hummingbird shadows. The scent of fresh lilac and rose danced in the air.

As she got closer, she saw a vase with a long-stemmed yellow rose—her favorite. How had he even found fresh flowers?

Dustin stood next to the table, wearing a navy suit jacket, sleeves rolled up, his hair combed neatly to the side, beard trimmed. He was playing guitar, and a man behind him began to sing.

We watched the lights go out one by one
We saw the last train ride away
Right then, we knew, our life had begun
We knew, together, we would stay

Anna's eyes watered. It was a song from her childhood; she'd only sung it to him once before, on the date when he played her his guitar for her for the first time. She moved to the music, mouthing the words.

The Red Rocks

All night we looked at blissful stars
The sky, told us, morning's not far
Who knew that we would meet this way?
Fate brought us here, this summer day

We knew that peace would soon appear
No more loneliness, or fear
We held each other tight and laughed
This was the perfect chosen path

"You remembered," she whispered in his ear.

Dustin put down his guitar and picked her up. "I'd never forget." He brushed a strand of hair away from her face and they kissed and held each other.

"I have one more surprise for you," Dustin said, pulling away. He took her hands in his and bent down on one knee.

"What?" Anna's eyes grew wide. "Dustin, what are you doing?" Her hands shot up to cover her face. At that moment, the singer picked up the guitar and began to strum a light tune.

"Anna," Dustin started, and then cleared his throat.

"I know we've only known each other for five months, and I know this must seem crazy, but . . ." He paused as if forgetting what he was going to say.

For a second Anna felt that she should stop this, but the lump in her throat wouldn't let her speak. Heat permeated her body, and an electrifying joy radiated within.

". . . but nothing has felt this right to me for a long time. After I met you, I didn't want to stop being around you. I never want to stop being around you. I want to save you from dust storms and crazy bandits. I want to buy you champagne, and give you fresh flowers. I want to take you wherever you want to go, and stay with you wherever you want to stay. I want to give you the life that you want, the life you deserve. I love you more and more every day, and if you let me, I will love and care for you for the rest of my life."

Dustin produced a ring from his pocket; it shone bright in the dim light.

"Anna, will you be my wife?" His rugged features seemed to soften.

Blood rushed to her head, and she froze for a moment before responding. "Yes," she whispered and then louder, "yes, Dustin, I will marry you!"

He slipped the ring on her finger, then spun her around, kissing her through their tears. A band came out to play a congratulatory melody, and the butler opened the champagne.

"I love you," Dustin said.

"I love you too," said Anna, kissing him softly.

"This ring," he began, "it belonged to my mother and then to my first love."

"I'm honored." Anna brought her hand up to look at the ring, then she looked at him. Her heart swelled. "It's beautiful . . . everything you did today . . . it's beautiful." The ring was a bit lose around her finger. She spun it so she could see all the sides. The stone was set in a vintage princess setting, several smaller stones etched into the band.

"I held on to that ring for a long time. I never thought I would find someone to give it to. I never thought I would find someone I could love again." He took her hand into his. "You mean the world to me, Anna. I love you more than life itself."

They kissed again, refusing to separate. Then Anna pulled away and looked at the ring once more. The gold clasping her skin felt uneven, and she took it off to examine the inside.

"It's engraved," Dustin said when he saw her thumbing the inside of the band.

Anna squinted her eyes and read: *with you, I'm hole.* She smiled.

"I know 'whole' is spelled wrong, but I've already made plans to get it fixed tomorrow."

She laughed. "It's perfect the way it is." She placed the ring back on her finger. "With you, I'm hole," she repeated, frowning.

Dustin pulled out Anna's chair for her to sit down and then sat down himself. He raised his glass. "To us," he said.

"To us," Anna mimicked, but something in the back of her mind kept bothering her.

The first course was a dozen fresh oysters, smooth, sensual, and delicious, but Anna could not relax. She loved oysters—she hadn't eaten oysters in years, but right now, they looked disgusting. They looked wrong. They looked like she felt.

Hole, she repeated to herself. Jake's face flashed in her mind. Pain and darkness replaced happiness, and a timeline began to form in her mind, each event bringing her closer and closer to the truth. It was the same phrase Bill had engraved on his wife's ring: *with you, I'm hole. H-O-L-E. Hole.*

Devastated to her core, she swallowed the rest of her champagne.

"Are you okay?" Dustin asked.

"Um." Anna forced a smile. "Yes, I'm fine. I just got a little dizzy."

"I feel a bit dizzy with excitement myself." Dustin refilled their glasses.

Anna forced another smile, but the dryness in her throat made her gag.

"Are you sure you're okay?" Dustin asked, worry accenting his voice. "I have a dinner planned, but if you don't feel well, we can go home." He took her hand. "I'm happy to do whatever you'd like. There will be plenty of other nights to celebrate."

"No, I'm fine. I'm just a bit overwhelmed," said Anna, spinning the ring on her finger, then she picked up the newly filled glass of champagne and finished it all at once.

Dustin raised his eyebrow. "Are you *sure* you're okay?"

Anna slapped the table with her hand. "Of course! Why wouldn't I be?"

Dustin stayed quiet.

"It's just the champagne. You know champagne always makes me feel bitter . . . better. Ha! Better, of course better."

Dustin furrowed his brow.

"Really, I'm fine. F-I-N-E, FINE! I think I'm just a bit out of it, but I'd like to learn more about how you came up with this. Everything is so wonderful. When did you start planning this?"

"That night on the balcony, when that shooting star flew by, it was such a serene moment, I just knew . . ."

Anna saw that Dustin's lips kept moving, but she didn't hear the words. She felt deaf, numb, alone. Unable to think, she sat there and pretended to be happy, mechanically lifting her fork up and down, placing food she couldn't taste into her mouth. Inside, her soul was shaking, screaming. Her thoughts ran, one faster than the next, around an endless track.

She coughed, and took a sip of water, trying her best to smile, and react with nods and laughs at the appropriate moments, masking the rage growing within. She held the steak knife in her hand and fought the urge to bring it up to Dustin's throat—Bill's throat.

"Everything okay?" Dustin asked, looking at her grip on the knife.

"Yes, I'm so sorry, my thoughts got away from me for a second. This is all so sudden, but I am happy." She almost choked on her words.

"Anna," he frowned. "You would tell me if something was wrong . . . if I rushed you in any way . . ."

"We're fine," she said, and chewed a piece of meat. It tasted like cardboard.

Dustin looked uncertain.

"We're better than fine," she said and swallowed. "We're great." She raised her glass and they cheered. They'd be even better tomorrow, when she found out the truth.

That night, when they went to bed, Anna pretended to be too tired to make love, the thought of the act repulsed her. Once Dustin fell asleep, she left the hotel room. She walked around all night until she found a shop that caught her eye, and bought herself a little gift.

November 2062 – Present Day
Bill Vos – The Red Rocks
Las Vegas, Nevada

The next day, Bill woke up without a care in the world, and even though he was a bit groggy from the champagne, he was eager to make up for the night before. He was overjoyed that Anna said yes. The night turned out just as he'd planned, but he wished Anna had felt better.

He turned to Anna, in hope of waking her up with a kiss, but found her part of the bed empty. "Anna?" he called out, and then sat up, rubbing his eyes.

She was sitting in the red velvet chair across from the bed, her mascara smeared, her eyes tired. She wore an old ripped shirt and sweat pants—clothes he's never seen her wear. A half-empty bottle of whiskey sat on the table next to her, and she held a nine-millimeter gun in her hand.

"Hi," she said calmly.

"Is this some kind of joke?" Bill looked around the room, confused, until he saw Emmy's ring sitting on top of Jake's picture next to the bottle.

"Anna, I can explain." Bill's tone was soft yet distant, as he assessed the situation, remembering that his gun was in his holster, which sat on the nightstand closer to Anna's side of the bed.

"Talk." Anna pointed the gun at him. She was trembling.

"Anna, I swear I didn't know who you were when we met. When I found out, I wanted to leave. I couldn't."

"Couldn't? You piece of shit. You could've."

"I had to at least get you to Las Vegas, after the attack of the two men, I had to make sure you were safe."

"Don't you make this about me. Any decent human being would have left. You had plenty of time in Vegas. And I . . . I thought . . . I . . . you made me . . . and then we . . . and it's all a lie!" She smashed the wall behind her with the gun and pieces of plaster rained down.

"Anna, I meant everything I said. I want to be with you."

Anna laughed. "Do you even hear yourself?"

"I'm sorry—sorry about everything," Bill said.

"Sorry that you killed Jake—your friend—and then tried to marry the woman he loved?!" Anna shouted. "You don't fucking say sorry for that! How could you? What kind of a man are you?" Anna shook her head and her hair fell out of her bun.

"Anna, please, try to understand. I didn't mean for Jake to die. It was an accident. He attacked me and I defended myself. I had my knife out and—"

"No, don't you dare blame this on him!" Anna threw a cushion from the chair at him. Bill dodged it. A somber glint shone in his eyes.

"I promise you Anna, I didn't mean to—"

"You're sick! You're disgusting! You didn't mean to? It was an accident? Don't you have an ounce of decency?"

"Anna, I promise you it was. I had my knife out, he jerked to the side. I told him not to take it out of his wound. I didn't mean for this to happen."

"Even if that is true, you did kill him, you killed by leaving him out there to die!" she slammed a fist on the table.

"Anna, there is nothing I could have done. I fired my gun so Bobby would hear. I knew he would take care of Jake. I did what I thought was best by leaving."

"Best for who? For you?"

"Best for everyone around. I didn't want to fight anyone else."

"Why did you even fight in the first place? You already killed his father, why come back to Jake? Why did you not just leave him be?!"

"I didn't know it was his father."

"I don't believe you! Your words mean absolutely nothing to me. Even if it's true, you're still a cold-blooded murderer! How many people have you killed in your life? 10? 100?" Anna took the whiskey bottle and threw it at Bill, he ducked, and it shattered against the wall just above his head.

"Anna, stop! This is crazy. I love you and I'm not a bad person."

"Not a bad person? You're the devil. I don't know why I'm even bothering with this conversation. I trusted you, and you . . . you knew this whole time and still, you—How could you!?" She grabbed her head with her free hand.

"I didn't know who you were when we met, I promise. I found out when we were on our way to Vegas. I'm sorry, I should've told you, but . . . I . . . I was afraid."

"Afraid? Afraid of me?" She gestured at herself with her gun-bearing hand.

"Afraid of losing you."

"Don't you dare!" She squinted her eyes and cocked the gun.

"If you loved me, you would have left. Right after you found out, you would've left. But you're not a man, you're a monster!" she cried.

"Anna, I'm sorry. I was selfish. I thought about leaving, but—"

"But what?" Hysteria overwhelmed her voice.

"I fell in love with you. I couldn't leave. I thought that I could make you happy."

"What kind of happiness is built on lies and betrayal?" Agony rooted itself in Anna's eyes.

"I would have told you," Bill said, his tone a quiet sorrow.

"When would you? When we got married? When we had kids?" Anna shook her head.

Bill stayed quiet.

"That's what I thought."

"I would have," he said, as if trying to convince himself.

"I don't believe you. How can I?" Tears fell from her eyes.

"I don't know what else to say, Anna. I love you. I'm sorry." Bill looked tired all of a sudden. He looked resigned.

"There is nothing you could say. You killed someone I loved, and then you deceived me over and over again. You should've walked away when you had the chance, and now it's too late," she said. "It's too fucking late!"

"Anna, please, you're not thinking clearly right now."

"Why? Why did you do this to me?"

"I love you Anna, and that has nothing to do with Jake. I thought about it over and over, and it was fate that brought us together. It had to have been."

"Fuck you and your fate."

"I'm sorry I didn't tell you when I first found out . . . I will forever be sorry for that."

Anna sat, quietly.

"I'll do whatever you want me to do. I'll leave if you want me to leave." Bill started to get up.

"Don't move," said Anna. "I will fucking shoot you, I swear I will."

Bill moved back down on the bed. "Anna, I truly thought about telling you, but I wanted to be with you. I wanted to believe this could work. I've felt like this only once before, with my wife."

"Don't bring her up! She's lucky she didn't see the man you've become."

Bill's face soured.

"How could you think that I could possibly ever love someone like you—a man of lies and deceit, a cold-blooded murderer!"

"I didn't lie about loving you," he said.

"I'm sorry, but that's just not enough," said Anna, her voice tranquil, her eyes clear.

"Anna please! I love you so much, I love you so much." Bill looked at her, his gaze sad, apologetic, defeated.

"Goodbye, Bill."

September 2045 ~ 17 Years Ago
Jake Deen – Metropolitans
San Francisco, California

Jake stared at himself in the mirror, green eyes dull, hair oily, skin pale. *Happy eighteenth birthday to me!* He'd better make the best of it, he might not make it much longer.

He walked out of the bathroom into the dark living room where his roommate, Devon, was dripping murky liquid from a vile into his eye. They shared a small, old apartment, where the walls were cracked, the ceiling yellow, and the mildew smell overtook that of stale tobacco.

Ads for cheap groceries and second-hand clothing covered the streets outside. Drug dealers stole every corner that was ad-free.

"You gonna join?" Devon held out the glass tube in his shaky hand, his voice hoarse from smoking.

"It's ten in the morning," Jake said and brushed his sweaty hands on his jeans. It had been several days since he'd showered.

"Never stopped you before." Devon tilted his head up for another drop. "Woo! Now that's how you wake the fuck up!" He squinted, then widened his beady eyes, then threw his baseball hat on the floor, showing his shaved head.

I shouldn't, Jake thought as he went over to the table where Devon was sitting.

"That's the Jakey boy I know! Volt yourself up!" Devon laughed, showing yellow teeth. "Oh yeah, your dad called."

Jake looked up from the table. "What did he want?" The sleeve of his plaid shirt almost knocked over an empty vile of volt.

"He wanted to know if you were home."

"What did you tell him?" Jake pulled his hair back with a rubber band, did a drop in each eye, and lit a cigarette. He felt his pupils shrink, and then dilate.

"I told him you weren't here." Devon went over to a lockbox hidden at the bottom of their entertainment unit, and retrieved more viles.

"Good." Jake sat down on the couch, his heart hammering, pupils waning and growing, waning and growing. His mind felt clear. He was able to amplify his focus on pleasant thoughts, and push away all the negative ones. He thought about pretty girls dancing, and pushed away thoughts of his father. His body felt pleasant waves of warmth, as if he was swimming through jelly, or rather the jelly was swimming through him.

"He also told me to tell you happy birthday." Devon pulled Jake out of his daze and began rationing out the drugs.

"Yeah, well he can go fuck himself." Jake spat.

"Whoa bro, don't be all pissed. It's nice that he at least remembers. My old man don't remember shit." He shook the last vile and then put it down. "In any case, I'm going to re-up and then we're having a party. We'll be celebrating all day today." Devon raised his hands in the air. "Yeah!"

Jake cringed after taking a sip of flat beer from a can he located on the table. "Well, I better call in sick to work then."

"We'll make this party last, and you'll forget all about your old man and anything else that's on your mind."

"I like the sound of that." Jake grinned.

~ ~ ~

It was three days later when Jake came to, after dozing off for several minutes. Devon was shaking him by the shoulders. They hadn't stopped partying since Jake's birthday, and it was increasingly harder to stay awake.

"Dude, so will you go get it?" Devon asked, pupils changing from large to small every second—two pale sirens, wailing for help.

"Get what?" Jake coughed.

"The money, man." Devon rubbed his hands together. "The girls are all out, and we need to keep the party going, you know, finish on a high." He laughed at his own pun.

Jake looked over to his side and saw two young girls, half dressed, furiously puffing on cigarettes. They weren't so pretty, at least not in the state they were in after three days of partying.

"Come on bro." Devon pushed on.

"Alright, alright." Jake got up and went to his room to search for any cash lying around. "Really?" he said aloud to himself. "Did I really go through it all?" He picked up his tablet. His head was so foggy that it took him three attempts to spell his password right and check his balance. Overdraft, negative. *Fuck!* He pulled on his only clean pair of jeans and headed out the door without a plan. "I'll be right back," he said.

"Get some beer!" one of the girls yelled as the door slammed shut.

That was the last time he saw them.

September 2045 ~ 17 Years Ago
Jake Deen – Metropolitans
San Francisco, California

Jake walked down the street, head spinning and mind set on cash and alcohol. He crossed his hands over his chest, pulling his leather jacket closer to his body. He walked without looking up, for fear of showing his shifty eyes. He thought a million times about turning around. He didn't need to keep going, he could end the party today, but every time, the claws of his addiction would make him take another step.

"What the hell is wrong with me? I'm supposed to be turning a corner. Getting better," he whispered to himself and kicked a small rock down the street. The more he looked at himself, the more he saw his father. He didn't want to end up like him—an abusive drunk. He wanted to finish high school, maybe go to college. Have a normal life.

He didn't have a plan. Not for his life—not even for right now. He rubbed his face with clammy hands. I don't want to come back empty-handed, he thought. He could steal—it wouldn't be the first time, but he'd have to choose a different liquor store—they already suspected him at the other one.

He took out a pair of gloves and put them on against the chill night air.

He couldn't believe he was going to do this. Disgusted with himself, he spat on the ground, but kept walking. He was halfway to the store, sauntering through a dark alley, when he saw a young woman walking toward him from far away. *Huh.* He looked her up and down. She looked small, but determined as she walked.

"She's by herself, maybe I can ask her for some money," he mumbled. He looked from side to side to ensure no one else was there. "Or . . . or maybe demand it?" He stopped and thought it over. He wouldn't have to go into the store and steal then. Less chances of getting caught, he thought. But what if she didn't have any cash? Well, she probably has something of value in her purse, or I can make her take cash out.

He was walking again. "I'm not thinking clearly, but . . . but what if this is my only chance," he muttered to himself. He needed to make a decision fast. He would need something to scare her. A weapon of some kind. He fished around in his jacket pocket and his fingers brushed against a familiar object. His pocket knife, perfect!

The girl was getting closer and closer. Jake took a deep breath. "Ma'am?" he said, when she was a few feet away. She looked up, but kept walking.

"Ma'am?" he said again, louder this time, and started following her, after she passed him. When she didn't look up the second time, he grabbed her shoulder, and she turned around. Jake noticed then that she was wearing headphones.

"May I help you?" she asked, taking out an ear piece.

Jake gathered all of his courage. "Give me your purse," he said.

"What?" Her face showed repulsion, her eyes a hint of fear.

"I said, give me your purse." He pointed to her large black bag.

"No!" she yelled and tried to run, but his grip on her shoulder hardened and with the other hand, he took his knife out. She cried for help, turned around, and swung her purse at him with all her might.

He ducked just in time, then popped back up to find her wielding pepper spray. He closed his eyes, but the fiery mist seeped through his twitchy eyelids.

"You bitch!" he roared and jabbed his knife in front of him.

Swoosh. Once.

"Stop!" The girl shrieked.

Swoosh. Twice. Jake felt he was losing control of himself. What was he doing?

Swoo—

"Aaaaaaah!" The third attempt was answered with a scream. Jake let go and opened his eyes through the burn. The handle was in the meat of her thigh. Jake grabbed and tried to pull the knife out, but it was in too deep. Her pants soaked through with blood in seconds. "Ma'am, I'm sorry, I didn't mean . . . I didn't want . . . I . . ."

She started to tremble. "What did you do?" she said, and sat down on the pavement, her back against the brick wall of the alley. He stood frozen. "Call an ambulance!" she commanded, and he could see a trying red puddle forming underneath her. "Take my whole purse, just call an ambulance," she pleaded.

Jake was in shock; he slowly picked up her purse and rummaged for a phone. He didn't know what he was doing.

Should he run? Should he stay? He was terrified, but not as much as she was.

"I'm so sorry," he kept saying, and felt warm drops sprinkle his cheeks. He realized that they were his tears. He wasn't sure how much time had passed, but every moment felt painfully long. His fingers fumbled with her phone and finally dialed 911. He placed the phone carefully between her ear and shoulder and put it on speaker.

He wanted to stay, but instead he grabbed the wallet from her purse, and ran.

~ ~ ~

When Jake thought he had run far enough away from the bleeding girl, he stopped and sat behind a dumpster in a dark parking lot. It smelled of rotten meat and grease. The air felt colder than usual. He looked down at his hands and noticed blood on his gloves. His body jerked and he closed his eyes. His mind hurtled over what happened, adrenaline rushed in, nothing made sense. He saw himself punch the ground, but he didn't feel it. It was as if another person was sitting there, someone he didn't know or want to know. Why had he done this? What if he hurt her badly? He needed to find her. He needed to know that she was okay. "Why? Why?" he kept whispering to himself as he rocked back and forth.

~ ~ ~

Several hours later, when he was too numb to feel anything, he took off the bloody gloves and buried them in the dumpster. Then, he opened the wallet and took out the contents. He flipped through the cards until he came across her driver's license. Using his phone to shine light on the picture, he examined the license. She was young and beautiful—eyes bright and full of life. She looked happy, she looked strong.

He choked up as he moved the light over her name. Her name was Emily, and next to her name, on a tiny Post-it, was a note. He mouthed the words, *"with you, I'm whole."* He put the license in his pocket. He'd call the nearby hospitals tomorrow—from a pre-paid phone—and see if she had been brought in. He could pretend to be a distant relative. They probably wouldn't be able to trace the call . . .

He heard a shuffle and saw a few shadows out of the corner of his eye. He started to get up, but before he could—*Whack!* And everything went black.

September 2045 ~ 17 Years Ago
David Deen – Metropolitans
San Francisco, California

"What are you doing here, Devon?" David asked.

"Jake's in trouble," Devon croaked as he pushed Jake's limp body through the door.

"What happened?" David took him and dragged him to the couch.

"He was supposed to go out to buy . . . food," Devon said and wiped his eyebrow. His breath was sour.

David scoffed.

"When he didn't come back, me and a few other people went to look for him. We found him in an alley, I'm not sure what happened, but he was passed out and bleeding. We think someone hit him in the back of the head. It looks bad. You should take him to a doctor. He might have a concussion."

"Thanks for bringing him Devon, now please leave."

David saw the blood-stained clothes and got Jake out of them. *What did you get yourself into this time?* He carried the soiled mess to the laundry. Before he dropped the jeans in the wash, he checked the pockets and found an ID of a pretty girl. Too old to be a girlfriend, David thought. He had a sinking feeling. He's in trouble. I need to protect him. David walked over to Jake and kneeled next to the couch. "Jake, whatever you did, I'll take the blame," David said quietly and patted Jake's face with a wet towel. This is my chance to step up and act like a real father. And I will.

David took Jake to a friend who was a nurse. They stayed at her house for two days, while she took care of Jake. She had stitched Jake up and gave him medicine, but he was still in and out. She said if he doesn't come to in the next day or so, he might have permanent damage to his brain. She urged David to take Jake to the hospital, but a hospital meant doctors. It meant jail.

On day three, when David was watching the news, the newscaster spoke about a robbery gone bad. The pretty girl's face was on the screen. She did not make it.

David turned off the TV when he saw Jake meander out of the room he was staying in. "What happened to me yesterday?" Jake asked and reached for a glass of water on the coffee table. His nose was swollen and accented by two black eyes.

"Yesterday?" He means three days ago, David thought and scratched his head. "What do you remember?"

"I don't remember anything and my head is killing me. What happened?" Jake moved around the room, smoking a cigarette. He touched the back of his head. "What happened?" he asked again.

"You really don't remember? You were at Devon's and then you went to get groceries." David thought it best not to elaborate.

"Did I?" Jake shook his head. "I thought I was there, but then I woke up here. I know we took volt and drank, but what happened to my head?"

"It doesn't matter now. What matters is that we pack you up and get you to the Red Rocks." David knew the way this sounded to Jake—like he was tired of Jake's shit and he was sending him away. It was the best way he could've handled the situation without raising any questions. Jake was used to him acting like a shitty father, it was what Jake would expect from him, and that's the way David was going to play it. Deep down, David hoped that by protecting Jake now, he would make up for the years of abuse and neglect. Someday, he thought, I will come find you. And I hope, someday, I can earn your forgiveness.

March 2063 – Present Day
Anna Faroe – The Red Rocks
Grand Canyon, Arizona

Anna stood near the edge of a cliff, looking down at the tiny trees below. The wind picked up and caught her hair, making it flow like waves of the ocean. It had grown long, and was as dark as a moonless night.

She took a step forward and almost lost her balance; bits of rock and dirt flew toward the ground, disappearing before they reached the bottom. She could just end this now, it would be easy. She looked down and took a deep breath. She didn't know what else to do.

It had been four months since she left Vegas, and she had traveled far away, each day trying to forget, each day fighting the urge to end it all. She had loved Bill. Maybe a part of her still did. He should have let her go, but he couldn't. Even in death, he couldn't.

She had felt sick after she left, and when she saw a doctor, he congratulated her. He said it was a miracle that she was able to carry, and then handed her a card of a professional in the Metropolitans. He said it wouldn't be safe for her to stay in the Red Rocks in her condition.

She took another step toward the edge. There was no time left. She had to decide. She placed her hand on her belly. Bill had always wanted a child. He had fought with Emmy and it led to her death. *Will I be next?*

She shifted from one foot to the other. Bill didn't deserve his dreams coming true. With one step, she could take everything away. But she'd be taking away a life. A child's life. A life a part of her had grown to love. Was it her fate to bring a child into this world? To create light from all this darkness? No, she didn't want to give Bill the satisfaction.

She took a deep breath. She had to decide. She looked back at the path; it welcomed her to return to safety. She looked in front of her, the rocks glowing red, the space below inviting. *I have to.*

Another step.

About the Author

Born in Moscow, Russia, and raised in California, Elizabeth Povarova-Simpson graduated Cum Laude from Saint Louis University, Madrid Campus. She worked in marketing for most of her career, and always pursued her passion of writing inside and outside of the office. She currently lives in Sacramento with her husband, Brent Simpson, and two cats, Saba and Toro. You can learn more about the novel and author on The Red Rocks Novel Facebook Page at URL: https://www.facebook.com/theredrocksnovel.

Photo taken by Brittany Tobar

Made in the USA
Middletown, DE
27 February 2018